The

Hurricane

Suzi Quatro

NEW HAVEN PUBLISHING LTD

The Hurricane

First Edition
Published 2017
NEW HAVEN PUBLISHING LTD
www.newhavenpublishingltd.com
newhavenpublishing@gmail.com

Back cover photo©Tina-K Photography
Cover design©Pete Cunliffe
pcunliffe@blueyonder.co.uk

newhaven
publishing

The Hurricane

To everyone I need
Everyone I want and
Everyone I love
You know who you are
I am lucky to feel inspired
Every day of my life

Content

The Hurricane

The Hurricane

Miami Beach.

The hurricane was building up, middle of the ocean, no-mans-land, unseen, unheard... swirling round and round, building up energy, getting ready to pounce. No one saw it coming.

Waves pound sandy beaches... torrential downpour... exodus of families fleeing to shelters. Emergency services standing by.

Nucleus of hurricane hits... unrelenting... branches flying... cars playing piggy back... bits of houses floating down the highway.

Unleashed fury all around as the storm destroys everything in its path. Tree trunks do head on collisions into walls, bricks turn to dust, the world turns upside down.

Storm at its peak... freight train express hits town... debris everywhere.

Until finally...

Winds decrease... calm descends... nothing would ever be the same again...

The Hurricane

Chapter One

1981 Bocking, Essex

Alison, aka Alice, depending on who she was at any given moment - both names suited her, and both were used - sat in the sunlit kitchen staring dejectedly into her umpteenth cup of coffee. "Oh God," she groaned under her breath, "Is that all there is? Didn't Peggy Lee do a song about that?" She wondered what she would do with the rest of her day. Only 7:30 and already she was submerged in a blue suburban funk. She hardly heard hubby as he clomped his way into the kitchen kitted out in camouflage shooting gear, broken gun at the ready. Who could have ever guessed that this 'wild child', this 'rebel without a cause', would end up cooking joints instead of smoking 'em? Did I change or did he, she mused; but, in the tradition of one of the worst last lines ever to grace a movie, 'tomorrow's another day.' Quick as lightning she shifted her black mood away, jumping up to give her man coffee, determined that he would feel free at all times; which anyone who knew her well realized was an old tape playing, inherited from her mother who was a slave to her husband, her house and Alison, her only child. Sometimes it could be absolutely suffocating, and Alice had vowed she would never ever make her man, when and if she ever met the right one that is, feel trapped. And, by God, she never did: but what a price she paid.

"Goodbye honey, have a nice day," she purred with a smile on her face, inwardly cringing at the sickly sweet sentiment. Later, she thought, I will work things out later, as blissfully unaware, unimaginative hubby Harry bent down and gave her a whiskery peck on the cheek.

And there she sat with the morning sun streaming through the kitchen window of her ridiculously huge, ridiculously secluded, ridiculously old 15th century house, situated in the flat countryside of Essex, the 'Manor'; oh God, how she loved it. Since the moment she walked in the front door she knew this home belonged to her. Every secret passageway, the crooked floors, the cracked plastered walls, the timber beamed rooms, the ghosts - who had even more right to be here than her - that haunted the floors, the acres of lawn, the neglected fruit orchard endlessly rolling down the back of the property into the moat which ran around three sides, yes, how she loved it; this house was hers and hers alone. So, even though she was lonely with boring tedious predictable sweet Harry running off to shoot or disappearing down the pub, she was in her own way content, because one thing she had fought for was independence and, as she reasoned with herself in the wee small hours, that was, after all, what she had achieved.

Alison Heart, rock singer, rock guitarist extraordinaire. Although it was still an oddity being a female rock and roll guitarist, she did in fact walk through that door. She was the bread winner, she was the famous one, she could have anyone she wanted. She was Alison Heart, the new evolving breed of female. The kind of woman who could cut your balls off at ten paces with one flick of her intellect. In charge of her own sexuality, not on the casting couch but directing the action; oh yes, she was in control. Everyone looked up to her - yet she looked up to everyone else. Who could figure it? Ego the size of a planet and the insecurities to match. God, what she wouldn't give for a little balance in her life: one extreme or the other that was her curse. She could swear, scream and fight with the best of them, and yet collapse into her own womb, weak with tears over something as ridiculous as 'Beauty and the Beast.' Who could figure it?

Alison was having a little break, which meant there were no airplanes to catch, no brainless interviews, photo shoots, t.v. shows... nothing for the entire week, and this was her first day of freedom. Hubby was out of the way, ridding the countryside of pheasants, rabbits, and pigeons, and the entire day stretched out before her like an endless ocean. These were the moments she liked best, on her own. In fact, if the truth be known, she often dreamed of living in the 'Manor house' alone, though she would never acknowledge this in her waking hours; at least not until this particular morning... she sat, remembering her life, and thinking out loud.

"So, here I am, 30 years old, a hugely successful world famous rock-star, a woman in charge of her destiny, yes, miles away from Mom, Dad, my home, my friends, everything I grew up with... Oh my God, did I really do that, leave the security of all I knew, with nothing but a small suitcase?" she asked the blue tiled walls in her huge country kitchen. Nobody answered.

"Well, it either took immense balls or total stupidity... got a bit of both actually if I am being honest. Yep, suitcase, guitar and a pocketful of dreams out to conquer the world. My God what a crazy ride it's been. All I had was the slim chance of a record deal and my hopes and ambition. But I had made up my mind. I was going, I would make it, and I wouldn't return home until I did... just 17 years old, so green. What the hell did I know?"

The Hurricane

It was with these recollections that she began her day, having no idea what repercussions this soul searching trip down memory lane would bring. Ms Heart - too much heart, if the truth be known - was about to embark on a very personal quest, the road to self-discovery. She was about to open the floodgate called 'feelings', unpack the emotional baggage that she'd kept hidden successfully for a few years now, take a good hard look at herself and find out just exactly who and what she was now, where she was going, and what exactly she wanted out of life after everything she had been through in the past three years.

Deep in thought, Alison glanced up at the clock. Good God, had an hour really gone by? Well, she hadn't thought of those things for a long, long time. Trying to shake out of it, but not quite managing, she dipped back down into the nothingness of her youth. Funny, most people assumed that being an only child she had been spoiled with attention, and although she did get a lot of that, it was meaningless. She loved her parents, but they had always felt like strangers. And finally, yes finally, she knew the reason why. Alison had discovered the truth of her early life quite by accident while visiting home a few years earlier in 1978... then there was that other matter of the heart in 1978, ending in 1979 when the whole thing had blown up in her face, creating craters in her soul.

Being famous did not fill the empty spaces anymore; in fact it never did, not really. Nobody really saw her while she was growing up, and nobody saw her still; now they saw Alison Heart. "Boy, what I life I have led, and very few people know about it, boy oh boy oh boy... the media would have a field day." She looked up to the heavens and sighed.

"Shit, this is getting me nowhere."

Jolting herself back into the present, Alice slowly got up from her oak carved kitchen chair, threw away the last of the cold coffee, and said aloud, "Well, if I sit here thinking of whys and try to make sense of things, I may never get up again. Aaah! God damn it to hell." Who she was screaming at was unclear but at least she felt a little calmer; primal screams always seemed to do the trick: just let it all out girl! Alice then began her day, surrounded by her success and swimming in her bottomless pool of loneliness, wondering what the hell she wanted out of life. She just didn't know anymore.

Alison was climbing the slippery stairs to her memory and to her sanctuary, the bedroom, which would have been heaven on earth if it wasn't for Harry and his chainsaw snoring. Still, he was a devoted, passionate lover. For Harry, Alice was his one true love. He saw his boat coming in and jumped on, a passenger for life, 'passenger' being the operative word. Oh, Alice did throw a few jobs and imaginary positions his way, if only to try and make him feel useful. The truth was, they had hooked up before Alice had hit the big time, and for all her balls she was terrified of living life in the fast lane by herself. She wanted someone there, someone who would hold her in the night, hold her tight until her demons retreated to the corners of her mind; someone who would be faithful, someone who she could be faithful to; someone who wasn't quite as quick witted or as ambitious as her, and someone who worshipped the ground she walked on. And, thank the Lord, she had found him.

Funny how they were so close for so many years yet she had kept the secret of her true beginning - and those other matters of the heart - to herself. Nope, nope and nope, she thought. These things are my cross to bear, and I will not change my mind. There is no point.

Harry... My Harry... Well, that was what she wanted in a relationship all those years ago, and that was what she got, for better or worse. But now, oh how things had changed. This woman had grown beyond all proportions. Her talent had blossomed into acting, television, and radio; she had even written a hit West End musical, and her brain, although always astute, was now razor sharp. Her records continued to sell by the bucket load and in fact her last album, 'The Heart of Alison', had won a Grammy. Poor Harry was left wondering where the woman he had married had disappeared to... the truth was they just didn't fit together anymore. Alice had known it for the past few years but she was her mother's daughter after all. And she sure didn't want to go down that path this morning.

"Two horses must pull the load together," she'd heard her say, dozens of times. Divorce was a dirty word, and not to be contemplated. So she got through her days at home, writing songs, poetry, drawing pictures, looking through her old telephone books, and daydreaming, until it was time to go back on the road again. In fact, either writing or being onstage seemed to be the only time she came alive these days. Yet, in a way, they had settled into an easy companionship, and it kind of worked. As long as she didn't think... as long as she didn't remember... and how long can that scenario go on?

Alison lay down on the bed and looked at her various performance videos, which she enjoyed watching and critiquing. She was always trying to improve. Settling on her biggest award winning effort, she put it on the machine, lay back against the pillows, remote in hand, and began to watch. As the songs were unfolding, she couldn't help but go back in her memory for the inspirations. They were the best songs she had ever and probably would ever write. And, for the umpteenth time, she tried to figure out a way to say goodbye to Harry without hurting him too much. This was a game she had played many times, over and over, with no conclusion, a game she had been playing since 1978. God knows she had come close so many times, but always backed down at the last minute... he loved her so. But that was what she truly wanted: to be free, to start again.

But as soon as this thought appeared her conscience poured cold water on it. Try, Alison, try... you can make it work. He's a sweet man, he doesn't cheat on you, he loves you. And maybe nobody will ever love you like that again, and that's a frightening thought. Yes, even for this liberated ball busting female, some things never change.

Maybe no one will ever love me like this again; but shit, there's got to be more than this... And this time, Alison's conscience lost the battle.

"Damn it - I deserve better!"

And feeling like little Alison Meredith all over again, 17 years old, in a rage, screaming her intentions across the dinner table, she shouted at the top of her voice:

"I am going, yes I am, with or without your blessing..."

Then Alice gave in to the moment, fell onto the bed in an emotional heap of tears, and cried her eyes out, remembering everything that had happened in glorious technicolour. Then she got up, turned off the t.v., went to the closet, grabbed the first suitcase she laid her hands on, packed, and left.

Dusk came around the corner, settling peacefully on 'the manor' as Harry rolled up in his Land Rover with the day's bag of pheasants, blissfully unaware that anything was wrong. He was about to have a shitty day, a seriously shitty day.

Scraping off his wellingtons on the mud bar by the back door, Harry propped up his gun, then shed his shooting clothes, and wearing nothing but thermal underwear and thick green woollen shooting socks, he strode happily into the house, whistling all the time.

"Alice, sweetheart, baby doll, where are you? Hubby is home and ready for a little hanky-panky. My gun is fully loaded and my aim is straight and true."

Harry's one saving grace was his ridiculous sense of humour, and if he deigned to smile at you, he could light up your world.

Hmm, she must be upstairs watching t.v. or something, mused Harry. I'll just dump the rest of these clothes and go up and surprise her in the nude... "Yep, that should do it. Better take my socks off though, boy oh boy, talk about a passion killer, she hates that," Harry muttered to the empty rooms.

He was about to find out just how empty the rooms were. Sneaking softly up the stairs, desperately trying to avoid the squeaky floorboards, he made his way to the marital bedroom. Opening the door with barely a whisper, peering into the darkness while his eyes adjusted, he leapt playfully onto the bed, immediately realizing there was no one there.

"Shit, where is she? God I am so horny too, just in the mood I was, shit, shit, shit," he muttered as he groped for the light switch.

As the lights flooded the room, Harry started to sense that something was not quite right. He noticed an open video case on the floor. It was one of Alice's live tapes from a concert that she was fond of watching, from 'The Heart of Alison' tour. A couple of drawers were slightly open, which was odd because Alice was ridiculously tidy, just like her mother; then, what was truly alarming was the closet where they kept their suitcases... that was open too.

"Hey, what gives?" It was then Harry finally saw the scrawled note on the bedside table. With a gut aching pain in his bowels, Harry read these words:

'My dearest sweet Harry....I tried, I really tried. This has not been an overnight decision... it's been going on for quite a few years now.... please understand......I DO love you, always will... just not in love anymore... I've done my crying, I've done my trying, and the well has run dry... I am going now... don't know where... will be in contact soon to let you know I am alright... don't hate me... you'll be fine... I will make sure of that... God, I am so mixed up... I need to go and find out who the hell I am... love' - and she had signed it with a huge A, and as an afterthought a couple of xx's, and then, because she wasn't through yet - 'PS there are some things you don't know, things that would help you understand me a little better... to understand us, things you deserve to know, and will know, eventually. Anon

 Alison xx
 Your Alice'

It was 3am and one of the brightest winter nights Harry had ever seen. Must be a full moon, he decided in his whiskey induced stupor. The log fire was roaring as he contemplated where his beloved Alison could be. Harry knew better than to alert the press at this stage: oh, what a circus it would be, paparazzi crawling over themselves in the haste to get the breaking story on the disappearance of the world's favourite female rocker. Yes, even in the advanced stages of drunkenness, Harry was nothing if not sensible. Besides, what was there to tell? Alice wouldn't do anything drastic, this much he knew. She loved life too much to be foolish. He had thought she had loved him too much to be foolish... yeah, like the old saying goes, you can live with somebody all your life and never know them.

The Hurricane

How long was it now - must be close to ten years - God, where had it gone? Harry got up on wobbly legs and gazed into the mirror over the fireplace. "Jesus fucking Christ," he moaned, "Who is this old man, and where the hell did all this grey come from, and these sunken cheeks, and these lines, I've aged ten years..."

This of course wasn't true. Harry had begun to age drastically about five years ago when he felt the love of his life, the woman of his dreams, whose smell made him go weak, whose smile lit up his life, whose eyes he could fall into forever, whose tenderness made him melt, whose strength amazed him, and whose neediness confused him, started to determinedly pull away from his grasp. His normality was always his ace in the hole, but now it seemed to spell his doom. Poor Harry, for he couldn't be anything other than what he was. This he realized, and to avoid the heartache he began shooting, drinking, playing snooker, poker - anything to keep him out of the house where every time he laid eyes on his wife he saw the cold hard truth. It was more than he could bear.

Now, at last, here was the day he had been dreading. Alice was gone... but where? Harry guessed he would receive a call soon either from LA or New York, two places Alice loved. And so he lit his pipe, threw another log on to the already blazing fire, poured three stiff fingers of whiskey and settled in the armchair next to the phone, ready for whatever awaited him. Harry felt, not incorrectly, that was the beginning of the end of life as he knew it.

Alison arrived at Heathrow in huge dark glasses, a baseball cap, track suit and trainers, topped with an environmentally correct fake fur coat. Ms Heart turned heads as she rushed to the ticket desk, somehow managing to be even more noticeable trying to hide than if she had been dressed in her usual stiletto heels, black leather mini skirt and skin tight t-shirt, booking the first flight out to New York. She didn't know why she was rushing, she shouldn't really, it was enough that everyone knew who she was; no need to call extra attention to herself by being a wacko.

"Thank goodness for Concorde, I want to get there fast today," stated Alison to the overwhelmed ticket agent, who was having difficulty concentrating once she realised her heroine, her absolute heroine, was standing right in front of her.

"There you are Miss Heart, the flight will be boarding in approximately forty-five minutes. Do you know where the Concorde lounge is?" she managed to stammer out.

Alice went into diva mode, becoming Alison Heart the celebrity for the briefest of seconds: "Really my dear, and which boat do you think I came in on? Of course I know where it is. Call ahead and have them open my usual bottle of Roederer Cristal please. Thank you so much." And off she went in a flurry of perfume and flapping fur coat.

"Gosh," sighed the agent, "What a star!" Alice hurried off towards departures, ticket and passport at the ready, heading straight for the fast track lane for first class customers, as a special services agent representing Concorde suddenly appeared out of nowhere.

"Good afternoon to you Miss Heart, can I just say I am one of your biggest fans and we are absolutely delighted to be carrying you to New York today. Please follow us and we will get you through all this palaver as soon, and as painlessly, as possible. We've phoned ahead and your requested champagne is on ice. Now, tell us what takes you to New York today, are you doing a t.v. show, recording, concert? Do you know that when I was a youngster yours was the first record I ever bought? To be quite honest, I did unspeakable things to your poster that was hanging on my bedroom wall... blah blah blah blah..."

Why did every male fan always have to share this information with her? Alice thought to herself, and at that point she simply tuned out and followed him through passport and security, then into the lounge, finally settling down in a quiet corner, hand luggage at her side.

Years of touring had taught her the advantages of travelling light.

She sipped her Cristal out of a perfectly chilled champagne flute, and, finally alone, contemplated the results of her actions.

Poor Harry will be beside himself. He didn't really do anything wrong... he was just being himself. I hope he's not getting too drunk tonight. God, should I call or wait until I arrive? I hope he hasn't called any press, or my parents, they will go absolutely mad. Am I doing the right thing? Shall I give it one more try?

All these thoughts raced around in her head as she sat silently waiting for the boarding call.

Maybe I should phone him, at least tell him where I am... Alice reached for the phone, dialled three digits and paused. She wasn't sure she would have any strength at all if Harry picked up the other end and started sobbing. Funny that, it used to be one of the most endearing things about her husband, the fact that he was sensitive and didn't mind doing the unmanly thing and crying his eyes out. Now, it had the opposite effect: she couldn't stand it, couldn't hear it anymore. Women are absolutely the stronger sex, she decided, and slammed the phone back down on the receiver.

He never would have had this life if it wasn't for me... the cars, the trips, the house, money in the bank. He had no ambition; a nice man, yes, but absolutely not needing to do anything spectacular. Just existing seemed to be enough for him.

What Alice forgot to add was that if it wasn't for her he never would have had this pain either.

"Right this way Ms Heart," Mr Special Agent - no wait, Mr. Special Wanker Agent - announced, interrupting Alice's trancelike state.

She forced a smile to her lips and followed, looking forward to three and a half hours of peace and quiet. Funny how life takes on surreal proportions when you're hurtling through the air in a cigar tube, eleven miles above the earth and at twice the speed of sound. She settled in her seat accepting yet another glass of champagne, Taittinger this time, a wonderful specimen of bubbly; Alice was quite spoiled by now and knew her wines, sparkling or otherwise. Hmm, she reflected, back to New York, well, that's where this journey began, and maybe that's where it will end.

And as Concorde screeched its way down the runway, shattering the countryside with its roar, she flew back in time. To a time when she was brave, young and fearless. A time when her dreams had an outside chance of coming true: up, up and away...

Chapter Two

Alison 17 Years Old

Alison had finally managed to extract herself from the tentacles of her mom and dad, but it hadn't been easy. Her poor parents just did not understand anything about her: never did, never will.

"You want to play electric guitar, oh my God, you want to go to New York... and join a rock and roll band with a bunch of boys called The Rough Edges! Oh my God what a name... and... alone? Alison Meredith Heart, what are you doing to your life?" This was from her crying mother. Then this from her father, who decided a threatening tack would perhaps be more effective: "Alice, if you go, you will never be welcome here again. I have not worked my entire life to provide for you and see you piss it all away on a hobby!"

Well, it took every penny she had, which was why she was now riding the Greyhound bus to New York instead of flying. She didn't mind; she never really felt safe in the air. Alice's favourite pastime was riding along in a car, gazing out of the window and dreaming her dreams.

"Yes... yes..." she muttered to herself, louder than intended. "I'm on my way. I'm going to New York City. Wow... I'm finally free, I'm finally going... Wow."

Alice was on her way to join The Rough Edges. It was her first semi pro band and she was beyond excited, if not a little terrified. Apparently the boys had been impressed with the tape she had sent with five cover versions, including all her favourite old sixties tunes, Louie Louie, Latin Lupe Lu, Twist and Shout, Do You Love Me, and her very very favourite, Jailhouse Rock... plus five originals. It wasn't great money and the hours were hellish: four 45 minute sets from 9pm to 3am. "God," she said to herself, "I hope my voice holds out!"

She was to rehearse for two weeks then begin a two month residency at the coolest club in town, Cheetah, in Greenwich Village. The boys were letting her stay in the apartment they rented in Chelsea.

It's probably a pig sty, Alice reasoned, but who cares, at least it's free. Now let's see: $200 a week, $75 goes home, which leaves $125, and all I gotta do is find food money. Shouldn't be too hard, I don't smoke, don't drink, don't do drugs, and sex... well, we'll just have to wait and see on that one.

As luck would have it, the seat next to her on the bus was empty, so Alice spread out, retrieved her song book from the backpack on the floor, and began working on some new lyrics. She always had to be creating: a song, a poem... the artistic spark burned strong and true in this teenage child/woman of the sixties.

She slept soundly throughout the night on the eighteen hour journey to the Big Apple. Trains, cars, buses: they always did that to her, kinda rocked her to sleep like the rocker she was. This ability would stand her in good stead as she would be 'on the road' from that day on.

The sun streaming through the dusty window woke her at 7am just as the bus was taking the exit into the city. Alice was immediately alert, glancing left and right, trying to see everything at once.

God damn, sonofabitch, we're going into a tunnel, hurry, hurry, get out the other side, prayed Alice silently to herself. Whoosh... and they were in Manhattan.

For Alice, who was a New York virgin, this first time didn't disappoint. It was everything she had imagined during all those endless bike rides she had taken back in Cleveland to use up the time. Big yellow taxis, honking, pushing, nearly colliding, scores of pedestrians jostling for position on the overcrowded sidewalks, steam floating out of manhole covers, street vendors selling an assortment of chestnuts, pretzels, hot dogs, ice cream... non-stop buildings, all crammed together, the new and old, the huge and the tiny. Wow, what a wonderland... Alice was hooked.

The adrenalin hit her smack between the eyes. You could smell it, you could feel it; shit, you could almost touch it. It felt exciting, dangerous, exhilarating and depressing, all at once. And a million miles away from Cleveland.

"I'm here, I'm here...Yes Yes Yes!" Alice shouted, turning bright crimson when she realized the entire bus had gone quiet and every head was turned in her direction. "Sorry. First time in New York City."

The Greyhound bus lumbered into the depot. Alice grabbed her backpack, her electric guitar and her small suitcase and disembarked, making her way to the information booth.

"Hi... could you please tell me which subway to take to get to Chelsea?" she asked the Spanish looking woman on the other side of the kiosk.

"Si, senorita, I can helpa you. I have zeese smalla map for you. It ees not deefecult, comprende?"

"Si, I mean yes, I see, si, whatever, thank you, gracias. Wow, this is great isn't it? Fabissimo!"

"Loco," said Wanita Perez, who after five years of handing out information to tourists from all over the world had seen it all. "Compleeeetely Loco."

She lit a fag, and went back to her true romance magazine.

Alice walked slowly; she didn't want to miss a thing. It was a typical New York summer's day and if she hadn't been so excited she would have realised how sticky and hot it was.

Oh my God, there's a Good Humor man, I wonder if he has toasted almond? He does, yippee... Alice took this as a good luck omen. Digging into her pocket for fifty cents Alice said to herself "Boy, I can't do this every day. I'm on a shoe string budget"; then she unwrapped her favourite ice cream, leant against the fire hydrant and wolfed it down. Finished, she wiped her mouth on her t-shirt making a greasy mark - shit, that is such a bad habit, I must stop that - and made her way down the cigarette strewn steps of the subway.

Digging into her jeans again for seventy-five cents, she bought her ticket, went through the turnstile, and boarded the train. Alice got out her map.

Okay, must be about here, Randolph Street. She made a big red X on the spot.

Finally looking up, she noticed there was quite a mixture of people on board: a couple of blacks, three Puerto Ricans, a tough looking gang of white boys, two nondescript young ladies obviously going to an office somewhere, a dirty old man who hadn't seen a real bed for a couple of years, and one middle-aged worn out looking woman with two bags of groceries between her legs, sweating profusely from her tent sized dress.

Alice was an astute observer of people, an expert at reading characters using body language and pure gut instinct as her guide. She was rarely wrong in her deductions, and all observations would eventually end up in a poem or a song.

She sat there silently, memorising every detail of her first day in New York. Just then, a gang of unruly boys started to slink her way. She quickly looked up and thank God, here was her stop... someone's looking out for me, she thought, that's for sure. Alice gathered her belongings and got off the train.

Okay, here we go; time to meet my destiny.

She made a striking picture at 5'5", thick wavy brown hair falling provocatively over one eye, slim hipped athletic body encased in skin tight jeans perfectly showing off her great ass, snakeskin cowboy boots, and black t-shirt covering just the right size bosom, yes, she turned heads wherever she went, even though she wasn't a classic beauty. She was more interesting than that; she had a face you could wake up to every morning and see something different.

Alice dragged along, looking for number 14.

"Okay, lets see... 3... 5... mmm, must be on the other side."

As she crossed over, she began to feel the heat as a trickle of sweat made its way down her forehead.

"10... 12..." Alice's heart skipped a beat. "14... here we are."

She dragged her guitar and case up the few steps, took a deep breath and rang the doorbell, once... twice... three times, in quick succession. Alice was not a patient person. The tinny speaker crackled to life.

"Awright, awright awready... which onea youse little creeps is ringin dis doorbell again... you kids is gonna get yo asses kicked but good... now ged adda here," said an unfriendly sounding male Bronx accent.

"Excuse me, my name is Alison Heart, I think I'm expected," Alice said boldly into the mouthpiece, bravado covering her nervousness.

"Christ awmighty... hey guys, it's her, come on, let's go down and welcome her properly. Be right there darlin... don't move."

Alice whistled, looking around, down the street that was to be her home.

Well, for the next two months anyway, she thought. If I don't like the band, the gig, the apartment, whatever, I can always move on.

Having an exit clearly signposted was essential at this stage of the game.

Just that instant, the door flew open.

"Hiya... hiya," said a tall gangly pony-tailed hippy.

So skinny, thought Alice. He must be the other guitar player.

"I'm Max, atcha soivice... I'm da one dat phoned ya. Ya must remember my sexy voice... irresistible, right! So, meet the rest of the bois: dis is Randy da drummar... dumb, but cute..." - Alice internally agreed - "Bobo, the real muso of da band, classically trained and all dat crap... and Harry da bass player... don't worry if you don't wanna laugh at his jokes; nobody else does."

Handshakes all around, and then they disappeared into the building. Up three flights of stairs, down a long dimly lit corridor, and finally they were there.

"Well, it ain't much Alice, but we like it. Welcome to da band, and welcome home," said Max as he bowed low, sweeping her into the room.

"So, who gets to fuck her first?" said Harry, with his usual inappropriate sense of humour. Nobody laughed.

Alice looked around, a blank expression on her face, taking in the ash tray full of joints, the empty beer cans strewn across the floor, a half finished pizza in a greasy cardboard box, sparse falling apart furniture, one couch and two arm chairs to be exact... and said:

"So, where do I sleep? Alone." She was looking straight at Harry, wanting to establish firm border lines for the future both verbally and physically. Harry stared back with a definite twinkle in his eye, taking the naughtiness out of his remark. They locked eyes. They were the kindest blue eyes she had ever seen. He was quite a big boy, cute in a cuddly kind of way, long brown hair, moustache, and sideburns.

Mmm, nice, thought Alice, as Harry's mean looking face broke into the most amazing grin. Then the sun came out.

For some unknown reason Alice found herself thinking: I've just met the man I'm going to marry; then she immediately wiped the ridiculous thought from her brain, and followed Harry into the small boxlike bedroom with a single mattress on the floor.

"Here you are darlin', this is your room. We even cleaned it out, see... no rats... in fact the only rat around here is me. But hey, don't you go laying any traps, I'm not as dumb as I look," said Harry. "But play your cards right, and you could have me," he added as he deposited Alice's things on the floor. "And by the way, you've got a great ass..." The door slammed. Yep, she thought, gotta marry that man.

Chapter Three

1981

Concorde was one and a half hours into the journey. Alice had declined lunch, not being in the slightest bit hungry. Her thoughts were running, fast and furious.

God, Harry, my Harry, my sweet, sweet man, where did we go wrong? I loved you so much, we were friends, lovers, we grew up together, then we grew apart, not without a little help of course... but I thought it was forever. Well, I guess that's the first lesson in life: nothing is forever. She sipped her champagne, not realising two big fat tears were trickling out from beneath her huge dark glasses. She was lost in her memories and more than a little tipsy from all the booze, with no food to soak it up. 'Nothing is real... and nothing to get hung about... strawberry fields forever,' Alice hummed to herself. Yesh, nothing ish real, nothing ish real... and nothing to get hunng abo... zzz... and then it was time to land.

Harry awoke with a blinding headache thanks to the nearly empty bottle of Glenfiddich on the table next to his favourite armchair.

"For fuck's sake, what's going on?" he grumbled, staring into the dying embers in the fireplace. It all came flooding back, hitting him full force in the depths of his soul.

"Alice, where are you?" Harry cried out, letting the tears flow freely. "Where are you my darling, are you okay, why did you leave me, what did I do wrong..." as he collapsed to the floor, fists pounding.

"Okay, stop it boy, pull yourself together, go upstairs, get a cold shower, take an aspirin, and make a strong cup of coffee." He staggered to his feet and cried one last time. "Why?" Nobody answered.

The five position shower head sprayed freezing cold water onto Harry's forty year old body, slowly shocking him back into some semblance of normality. He stood there for twenty minutes, until he was numb, then turned off the water, carefully stepped out of the tub and began to dry himself with an oversized dazzling white towel. In a daze, he went to the sink and began to shave, brush his teeth, and put his hair in order. This done, Harold Pullman, aka Mr Alison Heart, went back downstairs and made himself an overdose of caffeine, strong and thick, sat down on the dazzling white kitchen stool (Alice loved white, she always said it made things look innocent and new), and waited for the phone call that he sensed would come any minute now.

Wherever she went, he knew she should be there soon. New York was still his favourite hunch.

I gotta be calm, he thought to himself, cool, can't fall apart. Maybe she just needs a little space; take it easy Harry, take it easy... don't blow it by sobbing and begging down the phone like a wimp. She'll be back. But something in Harry's gut said this wasn't the case.

Lighting his fifth roll-up in less than an hour, Harry got up, paced around the smoke filled kitchen, and then sat back down, glancing up at the guitar shaped kitchen clock ("Just like the one my mom gave me, only bigger," Alice had said numerous times). It was 10 o'clock. Just that instant the phone rang, causing Harry to drop his cigarette.

"Hello, baby, is that you? Where are you, are you okay? I'm going crazy here without you. I couldn't believe it when I found your note. Why... why? What did I do, why did you leave me?" And against his better judgment, Harry began to sob, big gulping, girly sobs, sounding every bit as desperate as he felt.

There was silence, a long silence, and then, sounding as if she was next door, Alison's voice:

"Stop crying, please... this is hard enough as it is." Silence. "Harry, are you there?"

"Yes, I'm here honey, I'm always here for you. You know that. Talk to me... what's going on?"

Silence.

"Okay... I have something to say. Listen to me Harry, really listen. I've been doing a lot of soul searching lately. You must have noticed how distant I've been."

Silence.

"I guess there's no easy way to say this..."

Silence.

"I want a divorce."

Silence.

Alice was finding it impossible to stop her eyes from filling with tears, so she didn't even try.

Harry could hear her muffled sobs and took this as a positive sign.

"Alison... oh Alison, my Alice, I love you so much. You are my whole life... if you leave me you will destroy me. Please please come back. We can work it out, I'll change, I'll do anything, I'll get a job, stop drinking, stop shooting, whatever you want, only please baby... come back!" Harry choked out across the Atlantic. "Please!"

Silence.

"I'm in New York, at the Warwick. I'm okay, I'm fine, I'm fine, I'm fine... just a little jetlagged and a little drunk."

By now they were both crying hard.

Silence, sobs, more silence. Sobs.

"But baby, divorce? Come on, nothing's that bad. We love each other don't we... don't we?"

Silence.

"Harry, let me sleep now okay? Go to bed, we will speak in the morning. I can't think straight." Alice's guilt was tripping over itself. "Yes I love you, but sometimes the love changes... don't you see that? Don't you feel it? Now let me go. You know where I am. You know I'm okay."

Silence.

And this time, Harry wisely said nothing, waiting for Alice to hang up, and she did.

The silence was deafening.

She lay there for a little while letting the pain slide over her.

"And I didn't think I had any more tears left," she said softly into her wet pillow.

Then, realising she was overtired, she unzipped the secret compartment in her backpack, took out a 10 mg Valium, popped it into her mouth, and washed it down with the rest of the champagne, against every medical rule in the book. Fuck it, she thought.

"Okay, so I shouldn't be mixing the two things, but I'm not Marilyn Monroe and I haven't been rejected by both the president and his brother, so I should be okay, as long as I don't make any phone calls!"

Ms Heart had a strong tendency towards black humour when the going got tough. She gave a bittersweet chuckle as she wiped the tears from her face, and lay down, waiting for the pill to do its work. Her last thought before she fell asleep was Charlie Chaplin's famous quote: 'Comedy is tragedy plus time'... so maybe someday I will find all this amusing? Alice slept like a zombie for fourteen hours.

Chapter Four

Alice, 25 Years Old

Things were going well. The Rough Edges had gathered a loyal following through the years and were pulling in the crowds, and playing every night had really honed the band to perfection. They weren't brilliant, but they were pretty good. Well, they had been fine tuning their sound for nearly eight years, so they should be good by now; and at least Alice was getting lots of experience playing live, and writing lots of material, even if they did seem to be treading water. Of course Alice was the star, she knew it and they knew it, and after the first couple of weeks, Max had unofficially handed over the title of lead guitarist to her. He didn't have the same chops, never would. Of course, Alice being a girl guitar player automatically lifted the band to a different level, girl musos still being thin on the ground.

Harry and Alice had quickly formed a friendship which turned to love. They tried to hide it at first so as not to upset the delicate 'all for one and one for all' atmosphere, but it was soon obvious to one and all, discussed and accepted, and they now shared the single mattress on the floor in the little box room in the apartment in Chelsea. They were happy.

So... six days a week, 45 minutes on, 15 minutes off, 9pm-3am, pack up, off to the Stage deli for a quick snack, go home, a quick 'rumble in the hay' with Harry (or making love if you prefer), asleep by 5, up at 1, a late breakfast of toast and coffee, laze around watching t.v., smoke a few joints and get ready to start all over again. Except for the joints part, this was Alice's life, and she loved it.

Harry and Alice were having a very lazy Sunday.

"No gig tonight. Isn't it great honey, we have the whole day to ourselves," Alice said as they snuggled up close together, talking, napping, talking, napping. "So honey, how do you think the band is shaping up? Do you think we have a chance of getting a record deal, do you think we're good enough?"

This was the exact moment Harry had been waiting for. Although totally unambitious himself, he truly believed Alice could move mountains. Maybe now was the time to tell her what he had known from the very start. In fact, from the very first band practice, he could see that Alice had it - the X factor, star quality - she could go all the way. Mega stardom was in her grasp. He had nearly mentioned it dozens of times, but a fear of being left behind kept him from speaking out. But now, Harry felt comfortable enough in the relationship: he was hers, she was his - marriage, babies, the whole kit and caboodle - and so he began:

"Okay darlin', let's look at the whole picture. Max is okay, you know, just okay. The best thing he's got going for him is his sexy snarling looks. He's the original cock-rocker, and he does get scores of groupies hanging around every gig, so I guess he could go the distance, yeah. Now, Randy, well, his energy level is great but to be honest, his timing sucks... have you ever noticed how the tempo doubles every time he does a drum fill? And besides, I'm not so sure his heart is in it. Now, Bobo, what a crazy guy... don't you agree honey? I mean he's good, yes, and he's got the background thing happening, but Christ, he's such a pain in the ass, I mean he thinks his shit don't stink but his farts give him away."

Alice laughed out loud; she really loved Harry's sense of humour.

"I mean, even his name: Roderick P Weston... says it all doesn't it? Born with a silver spoon up his ass."

Alice laughed again, even louder.

"Shh! Don't wake everyone up! Okay, me, well, I may not be the world's best bass player, but I'm solid, steady, not too flash, kinda cute, with a marvellous sense of humour, and..." Harry was struggling to find more adjectives to describe his assets. "And... I can fuck all night!" That did it: Alice roared with laughter, not caring who heard them, and then, waiting for exactly the right moment, Harry added:

"And I love you more than life itself." They locked eyes again, looking into each other's souls in silent communion. Alice kissed Harry full on his moustached lips, drew back a little and said "Yes honey, united we stand, divided we fall," and then kissed him again with all the fervour of young love.

"Stop that Alice, I'm not finished yet. Let's talk about you. Do you know what you are, Alison Meredith Heart? Do you have any idea? You are a star. You can wipe the floor with all of us, we can't shine your shoes... you can make it big baby, you can go all the way; what do you say to that?"

Alice lay there, digesting his words, and in that instant knew it was so. She flew high as a kite, ego soaring, then fell into depression.

"But honey, what about you, what about us? You do mean 'we' can make it, don't you? I can't do it without you. I need you by my side. You're my man."

Harry looked deep into Alice's eyes, as if he was trying to read the future in them. He was testing the water but Alice was too much in love to realise it. She turned her head to the wall.

"Alice, look at me. You don't need me. You don't need anyone... don't you understand? Maybe I'll hold you back, maybe you will grow to resent me, hate me even. When you get rich and famous you'll be able to have your pick of men, the cream of the crop, not some slightly tubby, big lug of a man whose greatest asset is giving you multiple orgasms."

This was a serious poker game, and Harry was laying his cards on the table. He had raised the bet and now it was Alice's turn to see him or fold.

"Honey, if what you say is true, then I have enough talent for both of us. I love you and I want you here next to me, all the way."

And, for the moment, the game was over. Harry had bluffed and won, though deep inside he knew one day in the not too distant future Alice would hold all the aces and he would lose. For now, it would do... Sunday passed, and so did another joint.

Neither of them realised that the famous producer Mr Oliver Swift from London, owner of Crown Records, had been in the audience that night and he was impressed, so impressed that he attended the next night's show again, briefly introduced himself to Alison, who happened to be standing at the bar between sets, and handed her his business card. He said "Call me", and then walked out of the door without so much as a smile.

In the city, the weather had just turned from a liveable crispness to freezing cold; they even expected snow, although it was only the first week of December. The meeting with Mr Big Guy, Mr successful record producer, was set. Alison dressed in her best attitude clothes. She had persuaded Harry to let her go alone, knowing somehow that this meeting was going to change her life. She wisely didn't say anything to the band, not yet anyway. Her instincts were in full flow and she wanted to keep her cards close to her chest. So, dressed to impress, she went off for her date with destiny.

Mr Swift was of course ensconced in the presidential suite, and answered the door on the first tentative knock.

"Hello Miss Heart, very pleased to make your acquaintance properly. I'm Oliver Swift and I want to make you a star... drink?" he asked in well-modulated English tones.

"Hi. Coke please, the drinking kind that is. Well Mr Swift, that's straight and to the point. You don't waste any time do you?' replied Alice, surprisingly neither nervous nor surprised. Ever since she and Harry had had their talk, she was poised and ready, waiting for her ship to come in.

"So, what do you do then?" she asked mischievously, knowing full well he was the head of one of most successful independent record labels in the world.

"Well, my dear," the handsome, dark haired, dark eyed Greek god purred, in unsuited perfect Queen's English, "I make people like you famous." Then, looking her straight in the eye, he said, "Don't you American girls like to make love?"

Mmm, thought Alison, some kind of power game is going on here. Maybe he has the wrong idea because I came alone - damn, should have brought Harry along - wrong message received, so let's fix this misconception quick: on your feet, quick thinker. She retorted, quick as a gunshot: "Are you married, Mr Swift?"

"Ah... yes," Oliver spluttered.

"Are you happily married Mr Swift?"

"Ah... yes."

"Well then..."

They locked eyes for the briefest of moments, sipping their drinks, and in that moment they understood each other. There would never be another misconception between them.

"So, Miss Heart," Oliver Swift continued as if nothing unusual had occurred. "How tied are you to these boys? Would you consider coming to England to make a solo LP? I could do wonders with you, but

I can do nothing with them. You do understand what I'm saying, don't you?"

They locked eyes for the second time that evening.

"Maybe, maybe not. Make me an offer and we'll talk," this soon-to-be-rockstar replied.

Oliver, a little tired of the game, now passed Alice his business card again, and said: "Call me when you're ready to dump the losers and get serious." He gulped down his whiskey and soda, shook Alison's hand, opened the door and said "Thanks for coming my dear." The waft of English leather concluded the meeting.

Alice, returning to the apartment just in time for that night's gig, told an anxious and worried looking Harry "Meeting went great, will tell you later, no time, and I don't want to tell it twice, so let's have the band meeting after the show." She gave him a kiss, grabbed her guitar and strutted out of the door.

Finally the last chord of the evening had died, and the boys and Alice packed up their guitars and made their way back to Chelsea. Harry was the only one who realised what was coming. He knew something important had happened, could see it in her eyes, and couldn't wait to shut their little bedroom door and get the real version. He guessed it was only Alice who had impressed the English big shot. He had caught a glimpse of Oliver Swift staring up at her as they played with a predatory, greedy, shark-like grin plastered all over his face. And a good looking face it was too. Hmm, Harry thought, I'll have to keep my eye on the ball with that one.

Randy groped for the light switch and made for the couch, his usual seat, right next to the morning's leftover joint.

"For fuck's sake Randy, do you have to smoke that stinky crap all the time? It's bad for my nose and even worse for my voice," Alison shouted, more harshly than she had intended, for lying didn't suit her, not one bit. And she was about to tell a 'little white lie', but a lie nevertheless. She figured it was better to let them all down gradually. Damn, why did she always blush when she had to stretch the truth?

Max walked over and switched on the stereo, filling the room with the relaxing harmonies of the Mamas and Papas. He flicked open a can of Budweiser, and plonked himself down on the tatty armchair with the stuffing spilling out, spreading a fine spray of dust which mingled with the pot smoke turning it into a psychedelic snow.

"Cool," said Max, and took a toke before Randy hogged it all. Alice casually took off her duffel coat, shook out her hair and set her guitar in the hallway, trying to collect her thoughts on what and what not to say, for she knew they would want all the details before she retired for the night.

"Okay guys, listen up. Here's exactly what went down tonight. He said he may want to make an album" - (which was true) - "with us" - (which was not true) - "and he wants us to send him tapes, pics, biogs and stuff so he can listen and decide what to do. And now" - huge yawn - "I am tired, so we can discuss the wheres and whyfors in the morning. Okay, come on Harry, your woman needs some serious attention. Night boys. Don't get too stoned, eh?"

Once inside and safely cuddled up together, lava lamp glowing softly in the corner, they began to talk.

"Phew, that was a lucky escape honey. I didn't know what to say... you know, don't you? You know he only wants me. This is what you always said would happen and now it has. It's here, my big break. I can feel it in my bones."

Harry mentally noted that she said "my" big break; the word "we" was missing from this dialogue. He let her ramble on excitedly and tried to think what to say next. This was a delicate situation. He was the bass player in the group that was about to be relegated to the band who once backed Alison Heart. Oh my God, The Holding Company on repeat, bless Janis Joplin, Move Over, oh yeah. I just hope it's not going to be me who has to do the moving, he thought. Success for Alice was both his fondest dream and his blackest nightmare. He pulled Alison tight to himself, almost too tight, and felt her hard but feminine body mould itself around his body while he softly kissed her neck. She moaned, this being one of her erogenous zones; then slowly trailing down he stopped to suck on each perfect breast in turn. Alice moaned again, a little deeper, as he spent an agonising sixty seconds licking her stomach, then, finally, making it to the goal post. Alice was an oral sex freak, they both were, 69 being one of their favourite pursuits, and when she had finally muffled her orgasm into the pillow, he fucked her, really fucked her so her head banged against the wall and they were wet with each other's body fluids, bringing Alice swiftly to heaven for the second time, and finally... they were both ready for the finish line. Coming together was never a problem; then they were quiet. Harry got off his knees, doggy style being the best position, for Alison because it hit the spot, G, and for Harry because he got to watch her great ass as he pumped in and out with passionate thrusts.

"Wow, now that's what I call a fuck," gasped Harry, and he fell onto the mattress exhausted. Like a dog, he had marked his turf. She was his, now and forever, they belonged together.

"I love you baby," said Harry, slowly stroking Alice's silky smooth arm. "Let's go to sleep now, we can talk shop in the morning."

Alice slept like a log, and Harry laid there thinking, all night long.

Next morning Alice began to wake groggily, glancing at the guitar shaped alarm clock her mother had given her resting on the floor.

"God, it's 2 o'clock already," she said as she shook Harry awake. "Wake up honey, we have to talk, come on, wakey wakey you horny devil you."

Harry, who had only fallen asleep about an hour before, forced his eyes open with great effort.

"Mornin' darlin'. I didn't sleep too good. Okay, I'll grab us a cup of coffee and we'll talk."

Harry got up and padded naked to the kitchen. They were all close and nobody minded. He picked his way past the beer cans and bodies strewn across the sofas. "Well, looks like they partied all night long. If I stay up, I stay up," Harry chuckled quietly. He loved his sense of humour as much as his girl did. Filling the kettle, he switched on the stove, boiled the water till it whistled out of the little hole, and filled two cups with strong black coffee, which Alice was quite snobby about. She preferred the percolated stuff that hits you like a freight train going 100 miles per hour; low blood pressure, or something like that, she had said. He made his was back to their salubrious boudoir.

Handing Alice her coffee, he placed his on the floor and plonked himself down on the mattress.

"Come here baby. Mmm, you smell like you had some damn good sex last night, anybody I know? So, okay, let's talk."

Alice began: "Well, you know when I disappeared to the bar, that's when I met Oliver Swift. Nice looking man, huge ego, great accent and I would say more than a little dangerous. And he wants me, only me. I didn't have the heart to tell the boys. He wants me to dump the band. In fact his exact words were 'call me when you dump the losers.' He gave me his business card. God, where the hell did I put it?" She rolled off the bed, picked up her discarded jeans and shoved her hand in the pocket.

"Here it is," she said, holding it up to the light to read it. "Jesus Harry, get a load of this!" They both looked at the small black card with gold lettering. It read:

STAR MAKER EXTRAORDINAIRE   MR OLIVER SWIFT
'the fastest way to make your dreams come true'

"Is that an ego on wheels or what?" laughed Alice. "So what do we do now? We have to have some sort of a plan. When do we let the boys know?"

Mentally, she was already on the plane to England.

Harry, ever the voice of sanity, replied "Right, let's see how serious he is first, eh? Let's give him a call, reverse charge of course, and ask him to make an offer, on paper. Then, we find a good lawyer who knows about these things, and if everything is kosher, you and I will tell the boys together. And don't forget honey, when you speak to him you must insist it's us, you and me, we are a team, agreed?"

Alice looked up at her man. She saw the fear in his eyes. Kissing him softly on the lips she replied "Of course you silly man, just like we said, united we stand, divided we fall," and she kissed him again. "Now, how about a repeat performance..."

"You are insatiable, you dirty little girl." And Harry was glad about that, as he rose to the occasion once again.

When they had finished their quickie, Alice lay there feeling pretty good about things, until her mind clicked back to that last dinner at home when her mom was crying and her dad said "Actually Alice, you don't have any talent." She would show them!

A couple of weeks later Harry and Alice quietly slid out of the apartment down to the corner telephone box and dialled the operator.

The Hurricane

"Hello, my name is Alice Heart and I'd like to make a person to person reverse charge call to a Mr Oliver Swift in London, England, 5894928."

"Just a minute pleaaaase," said the whiny New York accented woman on the other end. "I'll try and connect you." Alice's stomach was doing flip flops. Click click... ring ring... ring ring... "Hello, Oliver Swift here." Silence... click click... "You may go ahead caller, the charges have been accepted."

"Well well, Ms Alison Heart, at last. Well, you took your time didn't you? You know one week is a lifetime in this business. So, what's going on, have you left the band yet?"

"Well, Mr Swift, I've been thinking, you see it's like this. I really do need to see something on paper before I burn my bridges. I mean, the boys may not be the best band in the world, but I kinda got used to eating regular."

Oliver chuckled. He liked this girl; she was different: ballsy, interesting, had something to say for herself. "Okay, here's what I suggest. I have to come back to New York again at the end of next week. What say we meet up at the Warwick and talk things through? I'll be staying in the Cary Grant suite."

"Okay, great, suits me fine. See you then. Bye," and the line went dead. "Boy, talk about getting straight to the point."

The Hurricane

Oliver went back to the dining table to finish his dinner. Greta, his wife of ten years, was waiting along with all his other possessions, between which he didn't differentiate. He sat down at the opposite end of their ten seater mahogany dining table set with Baccarat crystal and Asprey silverware and dinner service, surrounded by his many silver, gold and platinum discs. Everything he surveyed was there for the sole purpose of his own satisfaction. Oliver Swift could never be described as a romantic. He was a cold hearted and ruthless businessman, a killer who would relentlessly pursue his prey to the ends of the earth. He got what he wanted, and he wanted Alison Heart, though how he wanted her was yet to be revealed. Alison was right when she called him dangerous. He was a power mad, good looking, Greek/English Egotist; the Greek part won in the looks department, and the English part won in the class department. And he always got what he wanted.

"So, dahlink... who was that?" a deep boozy voice belonging to his wife enquired across the vast distance that was their dining area.

"Oh, some girl I found in New York a couple of weeks ago, guitar player, pretty good, smart too. I'm trying to sign her to the label."

That was all the information Oliver wished to share at this moment, so they finished their meal in silence. He was in one of his thinking moods and best left alone. Greta drained her glass of Chablis, and poured another. She used to be a very pretty woman, with typically Swedish long blonde hair, tall and slim, beautiful Nordic cheekbones. There was a time when Greta Folgel could have had her pick of the men. She chose Oliver. He had pursued her across Europe and eventually won her heart mainly through his constant persistence. That was fifteen years ago, ten of them married, and Greta was besotted still, yet had to live with the fact that her feelings were no longer reciprocated. Damn, if only she had been able to have children, maybe that would have kept his interest. The drink had done its dirty deed, and now, at 40, she was merely skinny, lined and sad. All her allure had been lost in the bottle, as she was, now, lost in the battle.

"Married alive," she said softly to herself, and drank another glass, silently toasting her handsome husband at the other end. "Cheers, you heartless bastard."

"So, what's going on, what did he say?" prodded Harry.

"I have to call him at the end of next week, at the Warwick. Then we're supposed to meet up and discuss things. God, honey, it's all happening, just like you said it would. Come on, let's get back to the apartment, I'm freezing my ass off, and I know you wouldn't like that would you?"

"Ooo, you little teaser you, I'm gonna fuck you silly tonight," said Harry, already half-cocked.

"Well, that won't take long then, will it?"

They hugged and ran all the way back to the central heating and the cold reception that would follow.

Chapter Five

1981, New York

Alison was slowly coming around from her Temazepam induced stupor. Little scenarios were dancing round her brain of times gone by. God, we used to be so happy, so in tune, but somehow, somewhere we got lost; we just got lost. Alice flicked through the t.v. channels, drifting back to 1976, the year she and Harry went to England... their private movie flickered across her mind...

Chapter Six

1976, England

It was January, snowing hard and freezing cold as the BOAC 707 left the runway at JFK bound for London Heathrow. Alison and Harry had waited, as was wise, until they had a watertight contract on the table, a small advance of $1000 (given in good faith), and two return flights to New York/London/New York, (all recoupable of course). Alice didn't like it but Dad had insisted she leave $500 at home to settle any outstanding bills. In the end, she figured it was a small price to pay for freedom.

The plane was shuddering and bumping its way into the sky, buffeted by the strong winds of a winter storm. She was nervous and forced her mind to think of other things. She thought about the band meeting. God, was it only two weeks ago...

Alison had finally decided that honesty would be the best policy. The boys were all ears as she began: "Here's how it is guys. You know I love you all and I've really enjoyed my time with the band, and I'll never forget you" - the air in the room was noticeably heavier - "but the truth is, I'm leaving. I've had an offer to go solo and make an album in England. In fact, I leave at the end of the month."

Shell-shocked, Max was the first to speak. "So Miss big goddam star... how's dem apples, so much for gratitude eh, little shit, who gave ya yer start? Who let ya take over on lead guitar even though I can blow ya off the stage? Who taught ya everything ya know? Max, dat's who, big Max... so you can take your stuff and get the hell oudda here, now..." Max stormed to his feet, spilling his beer and pizza all over the floor. "I'm goin' out for a little while, don't either of youse guys be here when I get back." He flew out of the door, nearly knocking it off its hinges.

"Well, that went well didn't it?" said Randy from his usual joint smoking corner of the couch. "I'm not mad at you Alison, I think you're great and I wish you all the luck in the world. You go for it girl, go on, make us proud."

He was such a sweetie; too bad he couldn't keep time.

Bobo said nothing for a few minutes, polishing his spectacles, then blurted out "Well, baby, if you need any scores done, you know, copies of your music, or if you need any really cool arrangements,

I'm your man. Glad to be of service to you." He turned his attention back to the television, already working out which auditions to go to. Bobo was a realist.

Alison and Harry went to their room and began to pack up their things. They had enough dollars saved to rent something cheap until it was time to go.

"So, honey, that didn't go too bad. Mission accomplished eh? I mean you can't really blame Max for blowing up like that. He'll get over it," Harry decided.

All this played in Alison's mind, which was busy busy busy trying to distract her from the fact that she was actually crossing the ocean in a cigar tube, until she finally dozed a little, and before you could say 'hit record', a loud ding signalled their final descent into London: tray tables back, seats in the upright position, seat belts fastened, touchdown.

Harry and Alice disembarked, following the horde through the terminal, too excited to be tired.

"Now remember what Mr Swift said, we're only visiting, not working."

"Yes, I know, I know," said Alison, trying without any luck to spot a bowler hat, an umbrella, a bobby, anything British, without any success.

Arriving at passports they joined the long queue for aliens, getting through without a hitch, and again they followed the horde towards baggage claim. Locating the right belt, they grabbed a cart and waited.

Finally loaded up they made their way through the customs hall - nothing to declare - then down the long lane teeming with hundreds of people on either side trying to catch a glimpse of whoever they had come to meet. "Keep your eyes peeled, baby," said Alice, "There's supposed to be a driver holding up a sign with my name on it. Look, I see him..." And she propelled Harry towards a dark-skinned man with a chauffeur's cap on, holding a sign chest high with a huge 'Heart' printed on it. "Look honey, he's got a heart on... get it!" They both laughed aloud.

Ensconced in the back seat of the Daimler limo, they both gave in to jet lag and fell into a deep sleep, so deep that the driver had to shake them awake several times when they arrived at their destination. Oliver had booked them into a small hotel in Chelsea, thinking Kings Road tube station would be a handy mode of transport. He didn't believe in spoiling his artists, and for the moment he was footing the bill. He hadn't liked the idea of Alice and Harry, but he relented when he realised that without him he didn't get her, simple as that.

Harry checked in while Alison surveyed their surroundings.

"God, everything is so tiny, and quaint," Alison said, sounding typically American.

She spotted one room with a t.v. and about thirty uncomfortable looking chairs against the walls. A sign overhead read 'guests only'. Nobody was watching yet. There was a tiny elevator just big enough for two people and to the right a staircase which led to the breakfast room.

"Okay doll, all set, let's go, room number 48." Harry opened the elevator door. "Squeeze in tight, we can just about make it. Fourth floor, here we are."

"Looks a little grimy doesn't it?" she complained, just a teeny bit disappointed.

"Well, I guess he's being cautious," answered Harry.

"Cheap, I'd say," retorted Alice, as they put the key in the door.

The room was minuscule, with two twin beds, a sink, a small wardrobe, and a window with a tiny central heating radiator in the corner. The bathroom and toilet were down the hall, shared by the rest of the floor. "Well, at least it looks clean; and hey, I don't know about you, but I'm gonna hit the hay, I am bushed."

Five hours later they woke up, disorientated and feeling like death warmed over.

"Christ almighty, what time is it?" mumbled Harry.

Alison checked her watch, adding five hours. "It's 7pm. God, we've slept most of the day. Let's unpack and get something to eat. I am absolutely starving."

Oliver, guessing they would sleep, had left a message at reception which read 'Welcome to England. I hope you have good rest. I will pick you up at 10am sharp. Bring any tapes of new songs, and your guitar. Regards, Oliver Swift.'

Chapter Seven

Back in Cleveland

Snow flurries were forecasted as the wind whistled across the storm windows at 1224 Elford Court. It was 10pm and Mom and Dad Heart had just gone to bed.

"So Arthy, our little Alison is on her way to England. Isn't it exciting? And I'm so glad she took her boyfriend with her. He's a very nice boy. I'm so glad she's not alone."

"Yup, she's on her way by now, probably about halfway across the Atlantic Ocean. I just hope she's made the right decision. She's so headstrong, off to New York at 17, now going 3000 miles away to another country. Yup, yup, yup, she sure is a tough little cookie," Arthy confided to his wife, begrudgingly.

Ever since Alison had told them the news of her contract with Oliver Swift, Arthy had begun to suspect he could be wrong about her. Hell, he thought, maybe she has got something, maybe I just can't see it, well, I guess I better keep my options open.

"Well, good luck to her. And if she does make it, she'll have to share the rewards a bit, won't she? After all, we have supported her every step of the way."

Mom thought to herself: Boy oh boy, talk about colouring the truth. As they fell asleep her prayers were for her daughter's safe arrival. Mom hated to fly.

One day, she thought, just before Morpheus arrived, one day, I will have to tell her who she really is, the whole truth. Yes... one day.

Chapter Eight

1976 England

The alarm rang on the guitar clock, and with great effort they forced themselves awake. Jet lag was the pits, for sure. It was 8am, time to get ready. Alison decided to wear her tightest pair of jeans, knowing full well her ass was her best 'ass'et.

"Always try and back into a room, that's my motto," she chuckled to herself. "Hey, honey, should I wear a little make-up?"

Harry gazed adoringly at the girl he loved. "Well, babe, you know I like you natural, but maybe just a little, like you made an effort... know what I mean?"

They took turns down the hallway sharing the bathwater, got dressed and went downstairs for poached eggs on toast and coffee.

"I'll run up and get your guitar, you stay here and wait for Mr. Swift," said Harry.

The Hurricane

At 10am exactly the sleek black and white Bentley pulled into view just outside the hotel's front door. "Phew," whistled Alison. "Get a load of that." Oliver was dressed immaculately in pressed Levi's, black Italian boots and a white cashmere V-neck sweater, completed with a belted mid-calf black leather coat, lined with mink. On his wrist was a diamond encrusted Piaget with a matching black strap. He made an impressive picture, his black hair, ever so slightly too long, blowing in the breeze. Dark Ray Ban sunglasses. He looked good, and he knew it. Taking the three front steps in one, Oliver stuck out his hand.

"Well, hello, hello. Nice to see you, and welcome to England. I hope you got some rest last night. Put your guitar in the boot and let's go."

Oliver kept up a barrage of friendly chatter, pointing out tourist sites along the way. "This is Cromwell Road, on the left is the museum of natural history... now we're in Knightsbridge, a very expensive area to go shopping in. Here's Hyde Park Corner, absolute mayhem most of the time... not far now... we're just off Park Lane, down Hill Street... here we are, number 11," he said, as he pulled over to the curb. 'Crown Records' the sign read on the semi-detached four storeyed house.

Oliver took them through the office, floor by floor, introducing his small staff of employees who helped run the company, until finally they got to the third floor, known as Oliver's retreat, which housed his personal assistant, Angela, and himself.

"Meet Alison Heart and Harry," announced Oliver, omitting Harry's last name, if he even knew it.

"Oh, super, how very nice to meet you both. Miss Alison and Mr. Harry. Welcome to Crown Records."

Hmph, thought Alice, perfect British accent, perfect lips, and perfect hair, and if she didn't have her nose so far up her own backside, she might even be pretty. She gave Angela her most dazzling hundred watt, melt the iceberg, super trooper megawatt smile.

"Gotta thaw this one out," she whispered to Harry.

Then, finally, they moved into Oliver's retreat, which was seriously impressive, from the chocolate brown Chesterfield set off by a perfectly pink natural marble coffee table, to the huge carved oak desk, with an inglenook fireplace in the corner, surrounded by awards and statuettes for his contribution to the music industry. Alison spotted one silver framed picture of a sexy young looking blonde goddess, who she guessed must be Mrs Oliver Swift. Then, recalling their first conversation, she wondered why he would even want to consider cheating on someone so pretty.

"So, kids, have a seat. Coffee?" He buzzed through the intercom. "Angela, please bring in coffee. Oh yes, and some of those delicious little chocolate wafers from Fortnum and Mason... thank you."

Lighting a huge Cuban cigar, leaning back in his chair, he began.

"I've brought you to England because I believe you have true talent. I didn't like what I heard musically, but I did hear something. You can be a star my dear." He was looking and talking only to Alice, making Harry feel distinctly uncomfortable and, even worse, unnecessary.

"Now, Alice, what I need you to do is to write me a hit song. Don't worry, I'll know it when I hear it, this is one of my talents. You did a song the other night that I thought went in the right direction, called 'I don't want to need you'. I like the twist in the sexes: don't mess with me, I'm one tough little lady. Stick with that, it suits your style and the way you look."

Alison wondered if that was a compliment or not.

Oliver continued: "All the other girl songwriters at the moment are soft and sweet, or almost too masculine; there is a nice position waiting to be filled by somebody who is right in between those descriptions, a gap in the market that you can and will fill. And you play guitar too, so that puts you in a very unique position. Your strength is in your maleness, encased in a very female body, in fact deliciously so, wouldn't you say Harry?"

Harry simply said, "Yep, that's my girl," establishing zero jealousy and ownership in one fell swoop.

"Okay kids, that's enough for today. Go on out, do the tourist thing, have some fun, and get some sleep. We start bright and early tomorrow morning, 10am. You can leave your guitar here."

Lecture over, Oliver went down the stairs.

Harry and Alison followed, more than a little bemused.

"Did you believe that!" exclaimed Alice as soon as they were out of earshot. "One song, he 'kind of' liked, one fucking song out of an entire evening of material. Gimme a break."

"Now, calm down honey. Let's look at the whole picture. This man has had ten years of worldwide success. There's just a chance he may know what he's talking about. So put your bruised little ego away and let's go and see some sights. Besides, tomorrow is another day." Alison thumped him hard on the shoulder. Although 'Gone With The Wind' was one of her favourite movies, the last line made her cringe, and Harry would use it to good advantage as long as they were together; which, at this moment in time, looked like forever.

Chapter Nine

1981 Bocking, Essex

Two weeks had passed. Two long lonely weeks full of lost days and lonely nights, fuelled with whiskey, cigarettes and coffee. Harry was miserable and spent his hours searching his memory for clues. "Where did she change and why didn't I see it?" he moaned to the empty kitchen. They had made one helluva journey together, and even though Harry was now relegated to tour manager, (he never did cut it on bass), he thought things were fine, well, fine-ish. Digging a little deeper, he realised things started to go wrong about three years ago. He had felt something shift, just wasn't sure what it was. It was the way she looked at him, as if she were tolerating his being there. Her kisses had become quick and dismissive, even when they were making love, which was increasingly infrequent.

So, he thought, what did I do? An ostrich... I stuck my head in the sand and hoped the danger would disappear. What an idiot.

The truth was, she had fallen out of love, or more to the point, she had realised she hadn't been in love in the first place. One man had taught her that.

She and Harry were in constant contact and spoke at least once a day. She was pleasant but detached. My God, thought Harry, what if she really wanted a divorce? What he would do without his darling Alison in his life, he simply did not know.

She hung up and lay quietly on her kingsize bed. She was in the Cary Grant suite at the Warwick Hotel, where she had first discussed her recording career with Oliver Swift, and it was in this room her life and her perception of love had changed three years ago. Only three years: it seemed a lifetime ...

Chapter Ten

1978

Alison Heart was now an established 'star' with four hit singles, two of them number ones, and a successful album behind her. She and Harry lived full time in London, in a nice apartment. Her life was filled with interviews, television appearances, recording sessions, photo shoots, and doing concerts around the world; she had very little time to herself. Harry was still her man but their relationship had become a 'comfort zone', faded, comfortable, like an old pair of jeans. The kind you can never quite manage to throw away. It was February and time to plan the campaign for the new single and album that was due out in April.

"So kids," began Oliver, pacing as usual, cigar in hand, "Here's the plan. We release 'Ballbust Her' at the end of March, then the album first week in April. We're sticking with the same title as the single, makes good marketing sense my dear. I'm sending you to Europe for a week to do some t.v. and interviews, then off to New York for the big press launch. This could be your biggest hit to date and I want everything in the right place. Harry, you will stay here, there's a lot of work to be done in regards to the tour."

This would be the first time since they had met that the two of them would be separated. Harry was dreading it; Alice too, though not as much. In a funny kind of way she was looking forward to a little space. They'd lived in each other's hip pockets for so long, it would make a welcome change.

Chapter Eleven

New York

Press Launch for 'Ballbust Her'

Alison was alone in her favourite place in the world, New York City, and for some reason she felt like taking extra special care dressing for the evening's publicity schedule. There was something in the air, she could feel it. Standing in her black lacy bra and underwear she began to apply her make-up, mascara first, then a little brown shading under her cheekbones. Staring into the mirror she decided tonight would be a red lipstick, black dress and spiked high heels night. For once she wouldn't go in her trademark outfit of tight blue jeans, cowboy boots and a leather jacket. This was her night and she wanted to outshine everyone. She ran her fingers through her wild mane of wavy hair which was now upgraded with high lights and lows lights making an electric mix of brown, blond and reds. Adding her favourite gold and diamond guitar necklace and her Cartier watch with matching Russian wedding rings, she padded to the closet to survey her wardrobe.

"God, I'm glad I thought to pack this dress, coz tonight's the night to wear it for sure..." A spray of Chanel No 5 and she was ready to go. Tonight she would take no prisoners!

The sleek black stretch limousine with the blacked out windows arrived twenty minutes late. "Stars never arrive on time my dear. It's important to make an entrance," Oliver had drummed into her on her way to the top. She swung her legs out carefully using her hand to keep the hemline acceptable, remembering why she didn't like to wear dresses in the first place, and faced the barrage of flashes going off one after the other.

"Over here Ms Heart"... "Smile please"... "You look wonderful Ms Heart"... "Where is your husband?"... "One more over here".... "This way please"... "Here Alison".... "Over here".... "Over here now".... sharks in a feeding frenzy, as the two gigantic bodybuilding bouncers led the 'star' into the hotel. The important people were inside, and for the next hour or so she would go from reporter, to DJ, to photographer, giving them each an exclusive five minutes. Lisa Gray, Rolling Stone's top interviewer, would get fifteen minutes, followed by a photo shoot for Billy Hayes, rock and roll's new golden picture-taker, which would be on the cover of next week's issue; then last but not least there would be a special television interview with king of the talk shows, Leo King, for NBC, to be transmitted that weekend, prime time, 10pm, Saturday evening, all across America.

Alison went into automatic, having done this numerous times, sipped a little champagne, and nibbled caviar. Yes, Oliver always did things with style. Rochelle, her press agent, monitored the questions and watched the time. It was her job to make sure everything went smoothly, but you were always guaranteed at least one asshole at these functions, she thought; and then, as if on cue, she heard "So Ms Heart, you've been with the same man for ten years now, how have you managed to make it last, you being so gorgeous, sexy and talented and him being, well... him?" This was said by a pimply, scruffy young man.

Alison gave him her famous 'look' and replied, quick as a flash, "Well, you being... you... should know the answer to that question. Oh, and don't hold your breath waiting for someone gorgeous, you'll probably die." Then she smiled a little to take the sting out.

"Okay guys, okay, that's all we have time for, thanks a lot," Rochelle butted in, taking her arm and leading her toward a private corner where Lisa Gray was waiting, tape recorder at the ready. She usually found female reporters a huge pain in the ass: bitchy and jealous, with misleading questions ready to trap her into saying something she never intended to say. But Lisa and Alison had talked before, and liked each other, so it all went smoothly.

Finally, she moved to the small back room where Billy had made a backdrop of red and white stripes to shoot the cover. He was a pro and believed in getting the shot quickly, which was fine with her, since she was beginning to feel the first waves of fatigue. Being 'turned on' could sometimes be the biggest 'turn off.'

"Hey baby, come on, sparkle for me, turn me on bitch, that's it, swing those hips... good, got it... legs a little further apart now" - (wink, wink) - "attitude baby, attitude, hip to one side, yes yes, I think we got it now. Phew, I need a cold shower, know what I mean?" And Billy Hayes was finished.

"Okay, sweetie," said Rochelle. "One more interview and then it's party time!" They both giggled, walking towards the rear of the function room, where NBC had constructed a makeshift studio with three powerful lights, a couch, a coffee table and two microphones.

Rochelle whispered into her ear, "Honey, now you gotta put your brain into fifth gear. Leo King is a tough, and I mean tough, interviewer. Some of the biggest, smartest politicians quake in fear when they come on this show. And, I guarantee you, he will be looking to crack your armour, so be careful. This is a big show for us. He doesn't usually do rock stars, mmmm, just don't let him do you, okay?"

Alison nodded. She wasn't worried; in fact, there was nothing she liked better than a little verbal volleyball.

Chapter Twelve

Enter Leo King

She saw him first, sitting on the couch, head down, studying his notes. A hairdresser was patting his greying hair into order. Leo looked up slowly until his eyes met Alison's full on. She felt as if someone had punched her in the stomach. Rochelle nudged her forward. "Mr. King, please meet Alison Heart." He rose and rose and rose, all 6'2" of him, dressed in a smart black suit, white button down shirt and black tie, about 58 Alice guessed, but trim and fit with it. His face was ruggedly handsome with thick dark eyebrows, full lips, a less than straight nose and the most electrifying black eyes she had ever seen.

"Well, well, well, Ms Alice Heart, Alison Meredith Heart to be exact, and what an absolute pleasure it is to meet you. Please sit down." He continued: "Oh my goodness, and in a dress I see, mmm, and high heels, most unusual for you isn't it?"

Alison blushed a deep red, and quickly sat down, desperately trying to understand what had just happened. She replied, "All for you Mr. King, all for you, enjoy!" The game had begun.

Leo King studied her intently, making a little small talk as the make-up lady powdered down her slight shine. Then someone shouted, "Ready to roll, attention studio, 5, 4, 3... 2......."

"Alice, may I call you Alice?" (Very few people called her Alice.)

"Of course... may I call you Mr King?" Eyes locked, they began.

"Let's start at the beginning. You come from Cleveland, I believe. What was your childhood like? Being an only child, were you lonely?"

"Yes, that's correct Leo. Cleveland, and the only child part too. So, lonely... is it real or just perception? And anyway, isn't perception nine tenths of the law! Yes I was a lonely child, but I certainly made up for it in my later years, wouldn't you say?"

The conversation continued. They discussed her music, her concerts, her poetry (how did he know about that?), her songs, and finally her views on love.

"One last thing before we have to wind this interview up." Leo King had made his name by zinging people with the unexpected, perfectly timed final question. "What is Love?"

The Hurricane

The entire interview had been building up to this final moment. It was a shame the microphones couldn't pick up the internal talking that had been going on since they sat down, X-rated for sure. Alison took her moment to think, staring directly into Leo's intense eyes, without wavering.

"Well, Leo, save the best till last eh? Okay, here it goes, I assume we are talking about true love, right? Not the minor ones we think are love until the real thing comes along. You mean L...U... V... LOVE..." (taking a line from an old popular Shangri-Las hit song) "Okay, here we go: it is... perplexing, elusive, confusing, annoying, joyful, tragic, uncontrollable, and" - Alison paused so long Leo nearly asked another question - "completely unavoidable. Same question back to you."

"And that's it for tonight folks. Thank you so much for being my guest tonight Alison. Please come and talk with us again," Leo concluded, successfully avoiding the question. He was a pro after all.

Never had thirty minutes gone by so fast. Leo had been uncharacteristically sweet, even giggling like a schoolboy a couple of times, and Alison had been soft and pliable, speaking in a low breathy voice, and so very honest. By the end of the interview, you couldn't get a sheet of paper between them, but flirtation between television host and subject was allowed, so they got away with it, just.

84

"So, what happens now?" sighed Alison, sorry the interview was over.

"Come with me, let's go get a glass of bubbly," said Leo, grabbing her hand.

The party was now in full swing and the guests were pretty loose. Leo plonked a dazed Alice down on the barstool then said in his best 'must not be ignored' t.v. star voice, "Bartender, over here, pronto, champagne, and none of your cheap stuff either!"

He handed her a glass, still holding her hand, then picked up the other one and said, "Well, my dear, shall we play with fire?" - clink - "Cheers."

They talked until the last reveller had gone, leaving only an anxious looking Rochelle and the two beefy security men. Alison and Leo were oblivious to anything but each other.

"What the hell is happening here Leo, am I imagining all this?" Alice asked, taking the first plunge.

"Well, I believe it's called being struck by lightning," he answered seductively sending delicious shivers down her spine. "But the question is, what are we going to do about it?"

"I don't know Leo, I really don't, I mean I've never been in this kind of dilemma before, and to be quite honest, I don't know what to do. My God, we don't even know each other."

"Don't we?" answered Leo, reaching deep down into her soul.

"Leo, listen to me, if we start this thing, whatever this 'thing ' is, I don't think I'll have the strength to walk away."

"So, my sweetness, then don't. Stay with me!"

"Only forever," she replied. The script was writing itself.

Rochelle walked over and interrupted. "Excuse me Mr King, your limousine is here; and Alison, we better be going, it's an early start tomorrow, you know, jet lag, beauty sleep and all that crap." (She'd had a couple of drinks herself). "I'll just organise our driver and we'll be outta here."

"Where are you staying?"

"At the Warwick, Cary Grant suite," Alice replied.

They stood and hugged, a little too long for strangers, and made their way back to their respective lives. Only when Ms Heart was safe in her bed did she allow any thoughts of Harry to intrude.

Leo King, top rated television host, 58, very married, four kids, six grandchildren, was visibly shaken, and stirred. He rode home in silence, deep in thought, euphoria giving away to futility. He was a cautious man, a few affairs here and there, nothing serious, and he was always discreet. His marriage was a very public one, 'the king and queen', as they were affectionately known, who, if not 'in love', cared deeply for each other.

In fact, Leo had always thought that falling head over heels was something that happened to other people, foolish people who didn't mind being out of control. As far as he was concerned the whole subject was forbidden territory. You lose control and you lose yourself, that's the way it is. His life was safe and in order. So what if he never felt that 'high' so many of his guests described when they spoke of their partners? Marriage was a compromise and as compromises go, his wasn't too bad, not too bad at all.

"So, why am I feeling like this if everything is okay? Ah, the unanswerable question."

Leo would be a very troubled man from this day on. When he arrived home he went straight to bed taking extra care not to wake Malinda who just might ask a question he couldn't answer. He slept fitfully, acting out the entire Karma Sutra with Alice as his willing partner, and the only thing that saved him from a 'wet' dream was his age, thank goodness, although 'goodness' had nothing to do with it.

Alison had tossed and turned and now it was 7am. Her wake-up call was booked for 8:30, but she knew sleep time was finished, so she got up and began her morning ritual: fifteen minutes of yoga.

While in the lotus position, humming her internal mantra, thoughts of Leo intruded.

I wonder if he'll call? And what will I say if he does? Concentrate girl, concentrate... hmmmmm, hmmmmmm.

Finished, she ordered freshly squeezed orange juice, coffee and croissants, turned on the shower, stepped in, grabbed the shampoo and started to sing, "I'm gonna wash that man right outta my hair."

Still singing and towel drying her hair, she heard a bell followed by "Room service." She put on the white terry cloth bathrobe and padded barefoot to the door, grabbing her wallet on the way.

"Thanks a lot," she said, handing the porter a dollar.

"Oh please, Ms Heart, anything at all, I am a huge fan, and can I just say how great it is to have you staying at our hotel, is everything okay, where shall I put the tray, when you're finished just call down, can I get you anything else, do you need a cab, how long are you staying with us... blah blah blah..."

"Yes, thank you, that will be all, you've been very helpful." She quickly shut the door. "God, is there no peace?" And just that moment the phone jangled into life.

"Hello, hello..." Oh my God, she never expected that voice on the other end, not at this time of the morning anyway.

"Hello my sweetness, how are you, are you okay?" Leo spoke softly into her ear as Alice's pulse began to race.

Pause.

"Hi. Well, it depends... if you call a bad tummy, a heartache, a confused mind, and virtually no sleep being okay, then I'm okay. How are you?"

"The same, absolutely the same."

Pause.

"Alice, listen to me," Leo blurted out. "I'm married, you're married, a lot of people are going to get hurt..."

Pause.

"Yes Leo, I know. So what do you suggest, older and wiser one, shall we walk away?" Alice asked, desperately trying to inject a little levity into the situation.

"I'm not wiser Alice, just older, and to be quite honest, I never thought I would feel like this, not in this lifetime, anyway." Pause. "So what do we do? The way I see it is right now, at this exact moment, we have a choice. One step further and we don't."

"Leo, I believe you're scared!"

Pause.

"No Alice, I am not a scared man. But I am dubious of what kind of a future we can have. We are both very public figures, the press would tear us apart, they'd hound us for the rest of our days. And, I think we both know, with us, it's all or nothing."

Pause.

Alice was beyond thinking, way beyond rational. She wanted this man, badly, more than she had ever wanted anything in her life. She was out of control. Delicious, absolutely... scary, absolutely... unavoidable, absolutely... oh shit! What is Love? Well, at least she knew his name now.

"I've got a full day today Leo and I'm confused and tired. I think we need to talk, away from the cameras and lights, away from our respective 'fame'. You and me, private and alone. It's too dangerous for you to come to the hotel, hell, they know me and they know you. Can you suggest anywhere, somewhere off the beaten track, somewhere discreet?"

Pause.

Leo was trying to make up his mind whether a meeting was a good idea, but his sensibilities faded into the background.

"Yes, Alice, I think we should talk. Can you meet me at Luigi's in Greenwich Village, tomorrow night, around 8:30, 45 Bleaker Street; and I think it's a good idea if we both dress down a little, don't you agree?"

"Well, if you like I'll wear a raincoat with nothing underneath!" Alice replied mischievously.

"Enough of that Ms Heart," Leo said gruffly. "I'll see you tomorrow."

"I can hardly wait... Leo."

The Hurricane

Click... conversation over.

Chapter Thirteen

1981 New York

The sun was disappearing behind the tall buildings of New York City. Alison was still lying on her bed, thinking, remembering, letting it all float through her mind.

"He broke my heart," she whispered to the shadows on the wall. "He swept me off my feet, promised me the world, and then, it was over, really over, with no way back. He's gone, he is really gone, and will never return... Damn, I should have known better to even have started something in the first place, but hell, when you've never had candy and somebody dangles a chocolate bar in front of your face, well, you just gotta eat it. It wasn't my fault, I wasn't looking to have an affair, and I certainly wasn't looking to fall in love, or... God, nope, don't go there. I was happy. I loved Harry. He was my friend and my lover. God, if only, if only... damn Leo, damn fate, damn everything. It's not fair!"

And, as always, when her mind got to this stage of things, she simply shut down. She couldn't and wouldn't go back there. Nope, it was done and dusted, over... onwards and upwards... with all these troubled thoughts she finally fell asleep, until a ringing phone intruded. It was Harry, a little tipsy and very upset.

"Hello? Oh, hi babe, God, what time is it? I must have fallen asleep," she mumbled across the Atlantic.

"It's midnight here. I'm sitting by the fire honey, and missing you so bad. Our house is a lonely place without you. When are you coming back darlin'?"

"Listen Harry, I don't know if I am coming back. Please don't keep pushing me. I have a lot of things to think about. Do something, get a job, get a life... These things happen. Just back off and let it be. I'm sorry if I sound a bit harsh, but you really do have to give me a chance here. What will be will be."

Pause.

"So, what do I do? Sit around and pick my nose? We're supposed to be a team, remember. What aren't you telling me darling? There must be more to the story than you're letting on. You didn't just all of a sudden decide I didn't make you happy anymore did you?" said Harry, quite loudly, beginning to fight back.

"No Harry, it didn't happen overnight. Tell me something. Have you ever loved anyone else?" asked Alison.

"Jesus Christ baby, what a question. You have been the love of my life since I met you. There never has and never could be anyone else but you."

Long pause.

"Well... I have..." The three little words dropped like a stone into Harry's heart. "And that's all I want to say at the moment. I will tell you about it when I see you. You deserve to know what changed me. Believe me, it was nothing you did. Just fate, life, chance... whatever you want to call it. Please, leave me be for a few days. Let me get to where I have to go. I'll be back sometime next week. We will sit and talk it all through and decide the best course of action for both of us. There is so much to tell you, so much I now want and need to tell you.

"I'll say it again, I do love you, I always will, I'm just not 'in love' anymore. Maybe I can live with that, and maybe I can't. Hell, maybe you can't... hell, maybe you shouldn't. Maybe you deserve more, did you think of that?"

Pause.

Harry was sobbing softly, trying to muffle the sound. He was so hurt. Picturing his darling wife with someone else was his worst nightmare come to life. He said nothing.

The Hurricane

"I'm sorry Harry, I really am. Try and get some sleep, and we'll talk in a couple of days. Bye."

Chapter Fourteen

1978 Cleveland

It was 10pm Saturday night. Mom and Dad Heart were full of excitement as they gathered in front of the television to watch their daughter's interview with Leo King. His show was essential viewing in the 1970s. For a rock star to command a half hour special was unheard of. This was an honour reserved for top politicians, best-selling authors, and maybe an academy winning actor. Yes indeed, she had truly arrived. Dad was taking no chances and had set up a portable television next to the big set just in case it went down. In his anxiousness he tripped over the wires, pulling out the plugs and causing set number two to go crashing to the floor.

"For Pete's sake Arthy, calm down, you'll give yourself a heart attack," said Mom as she settled into her favourite La-Z-boy, chocolate covered raisins at the ready.

A few annoying commercials played and finally the announcer said, "Now, stay tuned for the Leo King show."

"And now for the show folks..."

"Welcome to you all." Leo spoke into the camera, looking smart and distinguished. "Tonight we have something very special for you. We went to the press launch of 'Ballbust Her' and caught up with the very sexy and talented Alison Heart. So, won't you join me for this very exclusive" - (wink) - "conversation." Mom and Dad Heart were watching, and so were millions of others, as this undeniable flirtation began.

The director had been clever with the cameras, flicking from side shots to front shots, zooming in for close ups as the two of them revealed more than they intended. Alison's eyes shone as she blushed, stroking the armrests of the couch. Leo was obviously besotted too. His gaze never left hers and he had to pause more than once to regain his composure. You got the feeling you were eavesdropping on a private moment between lovers, and when it was finally over the lights faded leaving a shot of the two of them looking as if they were about to kiss. Leo couldn't remember what he had asked, and Alice couldn't give a shit about how she answered. They had eyes only for each other.

"I like Leo, he's good, but Alison was very different tonight, wasn't she? Not up to her usual quick repartee; and hey, what was all that about not getting enough attention at home? What a load of crap," said her father. "Well, it's not true damnit. She got loads of attention and I'm pissed off with her saying that, and on national television too. She's got nothing to complain about, she's famous, she's rich, and she's married."

"Well," Mom Heart said, "I'm proud of her. I thought she was wonderful. She's worked very hard and deserves every bit of success she gets. I'm tired of your crap. If I didn't know better I'd say you were actually jealous of your own daughter. I'm going to bed, goodnight."

Dad stayed prone on his La-Z-boy watching the news. Mom went to bed and thought deeply, trying to decide exactly what she had just seen. Was that her little Alison Meredith, good Catholic girl, married, loyal, looking like that at that old man? Something was happening, something serious. She'd never seen her daughter look or sound like that before. Should I mention it to Arthy or not? Mom wondered.

Maybe I'll call her tomorrow and see what going on, she decided, and finally slept.

Alison lay on her bed watching the show and sipping a glass of Chateau Beychevelle. She just loved French wine. She'd wisely left a 'do not disturb' on her phone, needing some space and time to digest what had happened, what was happening, and the full implication of it all. "Well, cheers to life saving situations," she said to the empty room, and took a sip.

The Kings had just switched off the television. Leo nervously cleared his throat, picked up the newspaper and pretended to read. His wife, Malinda said nothing. She got up, walked to the bar, took the champagne out of the bucket and poured herself another glass of Krug, then sat back down and lit another cigarette.

A few minutes of complete silence passed as she tried to decide what to say, if anything at all. The signs were there, and she was not a stupid woman. This Alison Heart has the power to ruin my marriage, she is dangerous, her woman's instincts screamed out from every bone in her body. She sat, she sipped, she smoked, until finally she heard herself say, "Well, my darling, if I didn't know better, I'd say you've fallen in lust," punctuated with a giggle, "Good interview though. Is she as nice as she seems?"

Leo looked up, feigning disinterest. "Hmm, what was that? Is she nice? Well, I guess so. Oh, by the way, while I think of it, I won't be home for dinner tomorrow night, got to see a PR man about an author he wants to get on the show, boring, boring, but it has to be done. Well, I am bushed. You coming up?"

"No, you go ahead, I'll be up shortly," replied Malinda.

Leo drank the last of his champagne and climbed the stairs. "Night."

Malinda's thoughts were running wild. What shall I do? Maybe I'm imagining it, after all, it was just an interview, and Leo always flirts a little with the females. But wait a minute; this wasn't flirting, this was serious. He doesn't look at me that way, in fact he never has... She sat, she sipped, she smoked. Well, we certainly didn't come all this way to be broken up by a mere 'pop star'. We have history together, children, and grandchildren. My God, girl, get a grip on yourself. Say nothing and it will pass as all the others have. Finally she was ready for bed. Neither of them slept well that night.

Alice awoke around 9:30, and stretched like a big cat, rolling her body this way and that. She had slept well and felt ready for the day ahead. I don't want to think about anything, I'm going to shop on Fifth Avenue, have a late lunch, and get my hair 'done' for a change, then come back and get ready... ah, but what exactly am I getting ready for? The question was rhetorical. "I wonder if I should wear something fireproof," Alice chuckled to herself, then fell to the floor into the first yoga position. "Hmmmmmm... hmmmmm... I'm not nervous. Hmmmm...

hmmmmmm... well, maybe just a little. Hmmmmmm."

Leo was up early, before Malinda, thank goodness. He didn't think he could stand a third degree. He could be very secretive but not in this case: it was written all over his face. He put on his blue silk robe with the gold initials LK on the pocket, went down to their enormous kitchen and made himself a strong cup of coffee.

I must be mad, he thought. What am I doing with this young woman? This is not a game we're playing. Maybe I should cancel dinner. No, why should I... we're not going to bed, we're just going to eat. We need to talk, that's all. Jesus, I've successfully avoided this situation all my life, now here it is on my doorstep. Well, there's really no choice. This is a journey I must take no matter what the outcome. But maybe it's better not to know...

Leo continued to argue with himself for the rest of the day.

Alison returned to the Warwick around 6pm loaded down with bags from Saks, Fogel, and Bally. She had really gone to town, new heels, new lingerie, new skin tight black leather dress and a new hair-do. On a whim she had waltzed into Vidal Sassoon and said, "Cut it off!"

Well, I needed a change, she thought to herself. Boy oh boy, Oliver will go crazy. Tough shit. He's made a fortune out of me. We'll just have to do another photo session, that's all, maybe this time Billy Hayes can do it. I'll call Oliver and let him know tomorrow. Hell, maybe I'll change my image completely. I feel different, why shouldn't I look different too?

Ms Heart began to get ready, taking her time with every detail. He said dress down, but I don't want to. I want to shine, I mean, we're not doing anything wrong, just having dinner, that's all. The message light on the phone was flashing, but she ignored it; Mom, Dad, or Harry could wait. This is my evening, she thought, mine and Leo's, and I'm going to enjoy every single second.

8pm finally arrived and she made her way to the lobby looking radiant, in fact looking exactly like a 'woman in lust'. The doorman bounded up to her and said, "Right this way Ms Heart, your taxi is waiting, and if it's not too much trouble, could I have an autograph?"

"Certainly," she replied graciously, and then she stepped into the yellow checker cab ready for her date with destiny.

Leo's day had been full of family, with his wife, eldest daughter Dianna, her husband Mal and their two children, Ruth and Rebecca. They spent the day by the pool watching the kids splashing around in the water. Last night's show only came up once when Dianna said, "Hey Dad, cool show last night. Alison Heart is really special isn't she? Hey, I think you've got the hots for her eh?"

Leo laughed, winking at his favourite child. "'The hots for her,' now what, pray tell, does that mean? A private education and that's the best adjective you can come up with!" he said, defusing the situation.

Outwardly he was calm and normal, exchanging small talk and pottering around the house.

Inwardly, he was petrified.

Should I cancel, should I go? He wondered, until finally it was time to get ready.

Leo quietly stole upstairs, jumped into the shower, lathered all over, got out, dried off, shaved, splashed on a little 'old spice' and went to the walk-in wardrobe.

Mustn't look like I'm making too much of an effort, he thought. Let's see, Levi's, good they've just been laundered and pressed (no creases of course), black shirt, black shoes, and black crocodile belt, and just so I'm not too casual, a nice Armani jacket over the top.

Satisfied, he went downstairs into the kitchen where Malinda was making herself busy cleaning up after the family. She'd been impeccably sweet and kind all day, having decided through the night to kill him with kindness, and show him what a wonderful irreplaceable treasure he had as a wife.

"Well, honey, I'm off, shouldn't be too late. Goodnight." Destiny had never been so busy!

Leo climbed into his silver turbo-charged Corvette and began to drive into the city.

"This is ridiculous, I feel like a kid on his first date," he commented to the black leather upholstery. "I'm 58 years old for Christ's sake, absolutely ridiculous." He pushed in a cassette of relaxing country and western music.

Finding a parking space he made his way to Luigi's, going straight to the bar and ordering a stiff martini. He waited. It was 8:45 before Alice made her entrance, looking wonderful as she strode like a star through the restaurant, turning heads every step of the way.

"Hello, my sweetness, you look good enough to eat," said Leo, rising up from the stool and kissing her on both cheeks.

"Hello Leo," Alison replied, taking in every inch of him. "Oh my God, look at us, isn't it funny, you dressed kinda rock n roll and I've gone establishment. I'd like a drink please, whatever you're having is fine."

The vodka martinis arrived at the same moment as the head waiter. "Would you like to go to your table? I can bring the drinks over to you."

"Yes please," they said together, anxious to be on their own. They were led to a tiny corner table, candle lit, private, and extremely romantic: just perfect. The waiter handed them two small menus and disappeared into the darkness. Neither of them spoke. Their eyes were locked in silent communication and the only sound was the electric sparks shooting back and forth. Alice lowered her eyes first, which was most unusual for her, and picked up her drink.

"Alice, I must tell you, I nearly didn't come tonight, but in the end I simply couldn't help myself. I had to see you."

"So, what do we do now, Leo?"

Leo reached up, stroking Alice's cheek, then her chin, then tracing her lips with his finger. "We do this," he said and leaned across the table, placing his lips on hers for the first time, slowly, deliciously, with the promise of heaven to come.

Alice broke away, her face flushed with heat, and sighed, "The hell with dinner, lets get outta here. Now!"

Leo got the check and they left, clinging together all the way to the car. They drove silently to the West Side where he kept an apartment, Leo's arm around her shoulder and Alison's hand on his knee. He parked, walked around to let her out, and led her up the stairs, into the elevator and up to number 816. He fumbled for the key, finally getting the door open, led her inside, shut and double locked the door, and pulled her into his arms. They kissed, hard, tongues probing, desperate to be united. Leo unzipped her dress, sliding it down over her boyish hips and perfect ass. She unbuttoned his shirt, and undid his belt, and his zipper, letting his trousers fall to the floor, until they were both naked. He paused, taking in her body inch by inch, his arousal obvious. But he was man of much experience and would not go off half-cocked. Then he picked her up and carried her into the bedroom, laying her softly on the bed.

"Alice, my sweetness." (He's called me Alice all the time, she thought, I never liked it until now... strange.) "It's not too late to stop. Are you sure you want to go through with this?"

"Oh Leo, I want you so bad, I've never wanted anything so bad in my life. I want you inside of me, now."

Leo entered her excruciatingly slowly, deliberately making her beg for more. They made love all night long, in every position, missionary, doggy style, on the floor, against the wardrobe, on the bureau until finally they collapsed in a heap, locked in each other's arms, and slept.

Malinda had gone to bed early with a Mandrax for company. She didn't really like sleeping pills, but she needed one. It was 6am when she stirred groggily, reaching over to touch Oliver and realising that the bed was empty.

What the hell, where is he? My God almighty I hope nothing has happened, she thought as she dialled the number at the apartment.

The phone rang, loud and shrill, instantly waking both of them. Leo knew who it was, and motioned Alice to be silent. He picked up on the third ring.

"Mmm... hello?" he said sleepily.

"Oh, Leo, thank goodness you're there. I've just woken up. I thought you might have had an accident or something. Why didn't you call me?"

"I'm so sorry darling, it was late and I didn't want to disturb you, had a little too much wine and thought it would be better if I stayed here. No need to worry, I'll be home around noon. Go back to sleep, everything is fine."

Alison lay very still, watching the conversation, taking it all in.

"Well, back to reality, eh Leo?"

"Shh. Don't speak my sweetness, just kiss me." They made love, tenderly, slowly once again. When it was finally over and they were both satisfied, Alison turned onto her side, curling into the foetal position, and said:

"So, what do we do now, what the hell do we do now?"

Leo was silent.

"I've got to be honest Leo, I think I'm in love with you."

He traced the contours of her compact body and replied, "Well, I suspect I'm in love with you too, and in answer to your question, I don't know what we do now. I'm as confused and as scared as you are. Maybe we should have a cooling off period, you know, think things through."

"Are you back pedalling Leo?"

"No, I'm trying to be sensible. I want you Alice, that's for sure, but like I said right at the beginning, I'm married, you're married, do we really want to rock the boat?"

"How can you rock a boat that's already been sunk?" Alice replied quickly. "Sunk by your torpedo I might add." She was trying to induce a little levity in the situation. "Look Leo, I'm only 27 years old. I have a future in front of me. I'm still optimistic. You're 58 which automatically makes you a lot more reluctant. I'm telling you now, for the record, I think I am prepared to change my life for you. I might even want to marry you. Of course I do realise I have to get divorced first."

Alison, always straightforward, no bullshit, couldn't see the point of beating around the bush and besides, she needed to know where she stood with this man who she sensed would hurt her badly one day. Well, I've never had my heart broken, perhaps now I will, she thought to herself.

They lay side by side until Leo broke the silence.

"I have an idea. I'm planning a trip to Miami soon to film a special t.v. show at the Excelsior. Why don't we go together? It would give us a chance to get to know each other better, and see if we want to take it to the next level."

"And what exactly is the next level?" asked Alison with a maturity beyond her years.

"The next level is 'forever', my sweetness, but now, I must make a move, got to go home. Think about it and let me know what you want to do. We could take separate flights and meet up there. Of course I'll pay for everything, but the booking better be in your name just to be safe. We can have a week of bliss. I would like that very much," he said, as he dressed. He bent over, kissed her softly on her swollen lips, and left.

Alison stayed another hour trying to decide what to do. She was married too, so why did she feel like she was the one skating on thin ice?

I'm the younger one here, she thought to herself, I should have the upper hand; I'm famous, good looking, no children, got the world at my feet, so why has he got me on the defensive? Okay, I will go to Miami. Maybe I'll find the answer there. This will be tricky: I'll have to work things out so it doesn't look suspicious... and for the second time in forty-eight hours, Alice contemplated deception, a word that had previously never been in her dictionary.

She got quietly dressed, and, after carefully peeking out of Leo's front door, she left the apartment. She hailed a cab back to the Warwick. She went to her suite, picked up the phone and pressed the message button. There were five waiting, three from Harry, one from Oliver, and one from her mother. She called Oliver first.

"Well, hello Alison, my little rock star. I've been trying to reach you, where have you been?" asked Oliver. "Rochelle called and said the press launch went great. Rolling Stone is very pleased with both the interview and the pictures, and I heard that the King show was positively super. You must be feeling a little tired by now."

"Oh, I'm okay. You know me, Oliver, I just go into automatic mode. But hey, now that you mention it, I am a little tired... might take some time off, maybe go visit my folks. Oh, and one other thing, I'd like to do a proper photo session with Billy Hayes. We really connected and I think we could create some magic together, and anyway, I didn't particularly like the last pictures we took. Maybe I'll change my image a little, you know, get creative or something."

"Oh, I see," said Oliver. "Do I sense a little mild flirtation here?"

"No, nothing like that, you know me, Sadie Sadie, married lady, I wouldn't dream of fooling around." (At least not until last night that is.)

"Well, I can't see any problem with taking a little time off. It would do you some good, a little r and r; that's rest and relaxation, my dear, not rock and roll," Oliver, who fancied himself a clever wordsmith, said with a chuckle. "Where were you thinking of going, if you don't mind me asking?"

Alice summoned up the 'actress' in her psyche... careful girl, careful; Oliver was a very intuitive man... "Well, now that you mention it, I would really like to go to Miami, catch some rays, walk the beach, and contemplate my navel. Oh yes, one more thing Oliver: I would really like to go alone. Do you think you could find a good reason to send me there? And don't go making a big deal of it - there's nothing wrong with me and Harry. I just want some space, okay? I will do Cleveland now though, and we can sort out a good time for Miami when I return. Not sure when I want to go, just sure I want to go. I need some space..."

Space? Now there's an interesting word.

That's the second time she's used it in this conversation, thought Oliver. That's always the first word out of a woman's mouth when a relationship has gone wrong. "Okay, let me give that some thought. Maybe there's something we can do on this end. Maybe a photo session with Billy Hayes eh... or was that what you had in mind anyway?"

"No, it wasn't, and stop being so nosey... and stop trying to second guess me. Yes, a photo session would be the perfect thing, but you will have to find something, something 'incredibly important' for Harry to do so he can't insist on coming with me. Will you do that for me... please? Anyway, no immediate hurry for that, it wouldn't be for about a month yet. Let's talk when I get back."

"Consider it done my girl. I'll see you when you return. Bye for now."

Click... conversation number one over. Now the tough one.

Mom Heart answered on the second ring.

"Hiya Mom, how are you? Hey, did you catch the show?"

"Oh goodness gracious, I'm so glad you called dear. Yes we saw the program. It was wonderful, and you looked radiant. We're so proud of you honey and we miss you so much. How are you? And how is Harry?"

The question seemed to have a hundred ton weight wrapped around it.

"Oh, I'm fine, just a little tired with all the press and stuff, you know how it is, same old questions, boring boring boring." She was trying to sound normal. "Is Dad there?"

"Nope, there's nobody here but me." Pause. "Honey, are you okay? Is everything all right at home?"

"Sure. Why do you ask?"

Mom cleared her throat. "Well... because I saw something in your eyes when you were talking to that... Leo King... and it's something I've never seen before."

"Well, what did you see, exactly?"

"What I saw, exactly," Mom replied in a stern voice, "Was my married daughter flirting shamelessly with an old man. I didn't raise you that way, Miss Alison Meredith Heart!"

Pause.

"God, Mom, you don't miss anything do you?" Alice chuckled. "Don't worry, it's all part of the interview game. Maybe I'll drop into Cleveland before I go back to London. I haven't seen you both for so long now."

"Oh, that would be so wonderful," said Mom. "Then we can talk, and I mean really talk. We are long overdue for a mother/daughter conversation aren't we?"

"Okay then, I'll make my arrangements and let you know, gotta go now. Give everyone my love. Bye." And they both hung up.

Something's up, thought Mom.

She knows, thought Alison.

And they were both right.

Chapter Fifteen

The Aftermath

It was 8:30 and the New York morning rush hour was building up nicely into the usual gridlock heading over the Manhattan Bridge into the city; fortunately for Leo he was heading the other way into the suburbs of New Haven, Connecticut - millionaires' row they called it - back to his safe, ordered, perfect existence. He was submerged in alternating emotions - guilt, euphoria, guilt, euphoria - keeping time with the windshield wipers as he cautiously made his way home.

"Guilt, now there's a new one for me," Leo said out loud to the empty car. "Up till now, I've always been able to do exactly as I like, and then walk away, but not this time. This is the big one, and I guess that's why I'm feeling guilty... and I guess 'feeling' is the operative word here. Do I really want all this 'feeling' in my life? Oh, I really am in the shit here, deep, deep shit." He slammed his hand hard against the wooden steering wheel, noticing out the corner of his eye a pretty young blond in a cream coloured Mustang, staring at him as if he was crazy. "Crazy, yep, that's what I am." Then, as an afterthought, he added: "Crazy in love."

"Shit, shit, shit, shit, shit!" And he drove the rest of the way home in silence trying like hell to wipe the huge grin off his face before he got there. It was impossible.

Leo turned off the main road into a private wooded estate which housed three families. They all had large five bedroomed homes set in three acres of grounds, and they all had swimming pools, yet none of them knew each other very well. This was a 'snobby' area, not your 'neighbourhood watch' kind of community. The sun was shining and a light breeze was blowing the cacophony of autumn leaves across the manicured lawns: yes, another perfect day in the perfect world of Leo and Malinda King. Leo shrugged his shoulders, put his 'happily married man' mask in place, and went inside.

Back in her suite, Alison finally dialled home. Harry picked up instantly.

"Hello? Alison? Hey, good morning darlin'... I tried calling you three times last night. Couldn't get you, got a little worried, were you out? I miss you so much."

Alison yawned. "No babe; I was so exhausted from all the press stuff, I put a 'no calls' thing on my phone and went to sleep. Boy did I need it, musta slept twelve hours straight through. So, how are things at home?" Alison was trying desperately to keep her voice normal, although normal was now something from another lifetime.

"Boring, without you. When are you coming back? You're through with everything now aren't you?"

God, am I really married to this guy? Alison thought. All of a sudden he sounds like a stranger. "Yep, all done and dusted, I'm out tomorrow. I think I get in around six in the morning. Haven't checked my schedule yet. Call Oliver, he has all the details. I may stop in Cleveland, though, and see my folks. I'll tell you all about my trip when I get back... gotta go now. I haven't packed anything yet - lots to do, talk later - miss ya, love ya, bye honey."

Click... conversation over.

Harry was left holding the phone. "Hey, wait a minute..." Shit, he thought, she's gone. She sounded a little strange, I wonder what's... ah, never mind, she's just tired, like she said. Great, can't wait until tomorrow. Harry whistled, walking out of the bedroom and into the shower.

Alison sat on the bed, still, silent, gazing at the wall, lost in her emotions. God, what am I going to do? She thought. What am I going to do? And as she packed her case, her mind flew back in time. 'When I was just a little girl, I asked my mother, what would I be?' The frequent memory intruded. This was a vision she had been having all her life: a beautiful auburn haired woman, appearing in her mind, always gazing down at her, always kissing, stroking, always smiling, and always the same song, singing, 'Que Sera Sera.' I can still remember the words, thought Alison. Damn, who is she? Is this a real memory or just my fertile imagination? Oh well, maybe I will never know: 'what will be will be'. She laughed.

The ringing telephone jolted Alison out of her reverie.

"Hello my sweetness, I wanted to speak to you before you left the country. Have you stopped smiling yet?"

"Nope, and I don't want to. Boy, what a night, but now I gotta go back home and face the music."

"And what music would that be my dear? Are you contemplating one last dance?"

"With whom, my husband, or you?"

"Either."

"God, Leo, I just don't know. I need a little time to think this through. Like you said last night, let's take it one step at a time."

"Hey, that's my line... now, what about Miami? Can you make it or not?"

"Well, I've kinda come up with a plan. I could go, just depends on when."

"It is being set up now, should be in about four to six weeks; I will have more information later on today."

"I won't know what's going on until I get back. My record company is arranging a photo shoot, a relaxing holiday, and a signwriting session for me and we just might be doing it in Florida, if you get my drift."

"Oh yes, I get everything about you my sweetness, drift or otherwise... so, let's keep in touch. You'd better phone the office, we don't want to cause any undue suspicion. Got a pencil?"

"Yes."

"Okay, area code 212... 6783343... let's say, every Wednesday at about 9am, my time, which is 2pm your time."

"That's fine with me. So you're a once a week man eh?"

"Hmm... You just get yourself to Miami and I'll show you what kind of a man I am." Wow, he sure knew which buttons to push.

Click... conversation over.

Leo replaced the receiver on the hook and sat at his desk staring into space. Luckily, his wife, Malinda, had been out when he returned, which was why he was able to sneak into his private study and call Alison. And as he sat there, his mind drifted back. So many women, so many affairs, and at the end of the day, what did it all mean? He never got caught with his pants down, and he always came back home, but most important of all, he never fell 'in love'... that was a mug's game. Control, that was the thing, to lose it was to die: keep the ball in your court, an ace up your sleeve, and never sit in the second seat from the dealer at the blackjack table, well, not unless you know the person sitting next to the dealer that is, and their cards number thirteen and they don't take a hit.

Mmm, he thought, I can still smell her... Just then, Leo's wife returned.

There was a sharp rap on the door. "Well hello, oh wandering one, Mr. Nomad of television. Do you have a hangover?" Malinda enquired cheerily. Oh yes, ignorance is bliss; even pretended ignorance.

"Oh, it's you. I was wondering where you were. At the shops?"

"Yes, I got in some smoked salmon. I thought we could open up a nice Chablis and sit by the fire tonight. How does that sound?"

"Sounds good to me. I'm just going to run up and have a shower, wake myself up a bit. You know dear, I just can't take those boozy evenings anymore. Completely knocked me out. Oh well, occupational hazard I guess. Back in a minute."

Malinda began to unload the groceries in the spotless, impossibly huge kitchen, a germ of doubt working its way into her mind. Then she had an idea.

Leo had neatly laid his clothes on the bed and was standing in a hot shower being pampered by the five different nozzles blasting him with water. He didn't even hear her come in.

"Christ, what the hell? Jesus Malinda, what are you doing in here? Can't a man have any peace?"

"Oh yes, a piece is what you can have, a nice big piece of me... Come on darling, we haven't done this in years. Don't you remember the first time we slept together? We went at it all day, if I recall, and to finish off, we did it again in the shower. Mmm, I can still feel you slamming me up against the tiles," she purred, rubbing her large naked breasts against his chest.

God almighty, he thought, how am I going to manage this again, and at my age? Better try though, or I will definitely have some serious explaining to do.

Grabbing the bar of soap, Leo thrust his hand between his wife's legs and began to wash her, rubbing, rubbing, rubbing, cleaning every orifice available, and, it must be said, visualising a naked Alison on all fours, begging him for more - and what a vision it was - a semi hard for sure, his imagination was never that good, but hard, nevertheless, ready for action once again. Ah yes, Mr Penis, the most honest organ on the human body, no conscience, either hard, semi hard, or soft. Better get this over quick while the dream lasts, thought Leo, and it didn't last very long at all. He just about got away with it, not so much rock hard, as rock limp. God, I hope she didn't notice. Of course she did.

Much later, sitting quietly on the couch like the old married couple they were, Malinda had time to ponder.

Well, she thought that was an interesting fuck, kind of somewhere between hard and soft. He was definitely hard for a minute or two, then down went the elevator. Something tells me he's been at it again... and I can just guess who that 'again' might be: Miss Alison, bitch, rock fucking star, Heart. Better keep a close watch on this one, she thought to herself, then said aloud, "Darling, do you know what I think? It would be a great idea if we took a little romantic break together, you know, away from it all. Sun, sea and sex, doesn't that sound nice? Don't you have a trip to Miami coming up soon? That would be perfect. I haven't been there in so long."

Shit, said his brain. "We'll see," said his mouth.

Chapter Sixteen

1976 England

It was their first year in England. Alison and Harry sat in the stifling hot little box room at the top of the Chelsea office of Crown Records.

"Phew, I'm tired. How long does Mr. Oliver - plum in his mouth, carrot up his ass - Swift, expect me to sit up here and write? God, honey, I am getting itchy feet, I need to put on my wandering shoes and do a few gigs or something, this is driving me crazy. I don't feel inspired, just perspired."

"Yeah, I know what you mean. Seems we had a lot more fun in the old days, eh?"

"God, remember the guys? I wonder what they're doing now... wonder if they are still gigging, wonder if they still hate me. Seems a million years ago doesn't it honey?"

Chapter Seventeen

The Rough Edges 1973

Max, Randy, Bobo, Harry, and Alison were doing well, very well actually. They'd been a successful working band for a few years now and were gigging like crazy, all over the States, in every godforsaken watering hole in the country. It was hard work, with a minimum of four sets a night, starting with a nearly empty club and ending with drunken revellers screaming for more. No record company had bitten yet, and without record success this was the circuit they were stuck in.

Alison was perfecting her stagecraft with every show, learning to deal with everything from idiot men who tried to touch, to uninterested drinkers who only came in to get out of the weather, or out of their minds, whichever was more important on the night.

It was in a gin joint in Saginaw, Michigan that Alison learned the art of 'self-defence '. The air was humid and heavy and the place was jumping. The band were getting lots of requests for their original material, which always pleased Alice more than the cover versions they were forced to do to stay in work. The Rough Edges were playing a steaming version of one of Alison's best songs, 'Don't Touch What You Can't Afford' when just in front of the stage some jerk with a crewcut started flailing his arms around trying to get her attention. When this failed to have a result, the jerk stuck his tongue out and moved it in an unmistakable oral sex motion, then curled his finger around his thumb and stuck the other hand's middle finger in the hole. Alison didn't stop to think, she reacted: she threw her guitar off her shoulder and whacked him over the head with it, then quickly put it back on, making it look like it was all part of the show. The jerk staggered and came to a stop, glaring at her, hatred in his red rimmed drunken eyes. The song stopped, the boys looked protective but nervous, and you could have cut the silence with a knife. All eyes were focused on Alison, so she stepped up to the mic, smiled sweetly, and said, "Was it as good for you as it was for me darlin'?" The audience erupted in applause and laughter. She added: "Thank you everyone. Going to take a little break now." It was over before it began.

Safely back in their kitchen/dressing room, Alison, soaked in sweat, flopped down miserably on the cigarette stained couch. "God, you guys, isn't this just too depressing? I mean most of the people weren't even listening to us, they were more concerned with getting totally out of their heads than enjoying the show. I mean I know this is paying the bills and stuff but shit, there must be an easier way to get to the top. And who can possibly do four shows a night, full power, foot on the gas, screeching away at the top of my voice, night after night, and I am so fucking sick of spraying that God awful stuff down my throat... ah, balls to it all, maybe I'll do something else. Maybe I'll be a nurse or something. Fuck it. Let's go home, Harry."

Everyone was unnaturally quiet after Alison's tirade. Quietly gathering their things they made their way home to the large, three bedroom caravan they were staying in on the edge of town, owned by the club manager and thrown in for free as part of the deal.

It was the first time Alison had spoken aloud her displeasure at the way things were going. She usually just put her head down and got on with it, but deep inside she could see no future for this band. The seeds of discontent were sown, and their roots went deep.

"Oh where are you my Svengali, my saviour? Come and find me, I'm ready..." Alice said, singing one of her favourite lyrics: "When you wish upon a star, makes no difference who you are, when you wish upon a star your dreams come true. God, I hope so!"

Chapter Eighteen

1978 Going Home

Okay, so you've had an affair, began her internal conversation. You've gone and done the dirty deed. And after being so damn good for so damn long. Shit, shit, shit. Oh well, can't put it off any longer, time to go home and see Mom. Maybe she can help make me make some sense out of my life.

She picked up the phone and booked a flight for the next day. She called Oliver to tell him her plans, and then she phoned Harry. She gave nothing away. "Just want to visit my folks; they are getting so old." And they were, but that was not the reason she was going home. She needed a reality check big time, and nobody did that better than her mother. She still hadn't decided if she was going to meet Leo in Miami or not; that was a tough call, and it would amount to nothing but lie after lie after lie, something she was not very good at.

The Hurricane

Looking out of the window, watching the plane touch down at Cleveland airport, all the familiar feelings rushed around, enveloping her in a feeling of wellbeing. Home is home after all. So, this should be interesting, she thought. I haven't been back here since I made it. I wonder how things have changed, I wonder if any of my friends are around, who's married, who has babies, I wonder how Mom and Dad are coping being the parents of Alison Meredith Heart. I wonder if my bedroom is still there. Now there's a thought: maybe she made it into a sewing room or something, who knows?'

The ride from the airport was pleasant enough sitting in the back seat of her parents' twenty year old Chevy wagon, with her few bags packed in the back, the radio turned low on her favourite radio station from her teenage years, and how weird: they started to play 'Ballbust Her'! "Turn it up Mom, just for this song please." Mom did. Song over, Mom and Dad kept up a barrage of meaningless chatter and a hundred and one questions. Alice let her mind go to neutral. No concentration was necessary.

Arriving finally at the small, clean, detached bungalow in the small, clean, 'detached' suburban street that she grew up on, Alison went immediately to her old room and was relieved to see it was exactly how she had left it. Aw, she thought, now that's nice. It's like stepping back in time. Think I'll unpack and wander around, get reacclimatised.

The Hurricane

The first night home was spent quietly in front of the family television, and nobody spoke much.

"Well," announced Alison, "I am turning in." She gave a glance at Mom. The glance said 'We can talk tomorrow.' "Goodnight everyone."

Morning came softly with the sunlight peeking through the yellow flowered curtained window and the birds singing their familiar song. Still asleep, Alison felt she was a child again. Here comes that pretty lady again, in a beautiful white dress, this time with a sunhat on. "Come along with me sweetheart, we are going to the beach today." She took Alison's hand... the tears came rolling down her cheeks, and then she was awake, at home, in Cleveland.

Just a dream after all... or was it?

Alison padded barefoot into the kitchen where Mom was busy making eggs sunny side up, crispy bacon and lightly buttered toast, just the way she liked it. "Boy that smells good Mom, bring it over. I am absolutely starved." Dad had already left for the day. Mom poured out the coffee, sat down and said, "Right, finish your breakfast, and then we will talk."

"Okay Mom. I know you have questions, not so sure I have answers."

"Now, Alison Meredith Heart, first of all I want to know what is going on with you and Harry. Let's start there. Are you happy?"

"Oh Mom, I just don't know anymore. I love him, sure I do, but I have more than a sneaking suspicion that I am not 'in' love with him anymore. I just don't know if I can live like that."

"Oh, for Pete's sake, is that all you're worried about? Don't you know that the 'in love' feeling goes after a few years, and then it's replaced by respect, trust, and honesty, which believe me are much more valuable commodities. Harry is a good man. He loves you more than life itself, and will be a good father to your children; that is when you finally have some," Mom said pointedly. "I sure wouldn't mind a grandchild or two now that I am getting on in years. And what's happening on that account? Why no kids yet?"

Kids, Alison thought, oh my God, kids, yes, I would have a houseful, if only it was with Leo... Thoughts and emotions were running around her brain. She looked directly into her mother's eyes, and saw that Mom Heart knew it all.

"I've had an affair, and he's married." There, it was said.

The silence was deafening.

Mom Heart looked horrified, then tried to rein it all in and look normal, which was not easy in the circumstances. Finally, she quietly said:

"I have a hair appointment, and if I don't go now I will be late. We will continue this conversation later. Why don't you just take it easy today, relax, and unwind. I love you Alison Meredith." And she left the room.

Alison sat there, in the empty quiet kitchen. Ah, she thought, home sweet home, nothing ever changes, the same plastic cover on the table, the same napkin holder, candles, kettle on the stove, pink wallpaper and pink kitchen towels, so orderly, so 'Mom'.

Right, so, what do I want to do today? Hey, why not go down memory lane? That's it, I will have an old photograph album orgy. I always did like that. And off she went to her mother's bedroom cupboard to get them all down from the shelf.

She settled down in her dad's favourite La-Z-boy chair with a glass of milk and some chocolate covered raisins, switched on the table lamp and began her journey. Flicking from page to page, she saw pictures she had looked at time and time again. Funny, she thought again for the hundredth time of looking at these family snaps, there are none of me as a baby, none as a tot. All the photos seem to start at age five... must ask Mom about that when she gets back, there must be a reason. Maybe they didn't have a camera or something? Or maybe they just weren't into taking pictures. But still, there must have been some taken. She kept viewing the pictures: school days, teenage years (My God, look at that outfit... look at that hair!), page after page, like watching a movie of her life... and then, omg, you could see it:

she found her music, age 12, and overnight her look changed. She had attitude, purpose, swagger... then came the appearance of her first guitar. She was 14, and boy she had to beg for that, and she managed to persuade Dad to pay for lessons too. She remembered listening to every single rock and roll record that had a decent guitarist playing on it... wow, it all came flooding back. She focussed in on one picture of herself, dressed in skin tight jeans and pink snakeskin cowboy boots and holding her low slung prized pink guitar. Yep, that's me! Then I was 17; and then I left home. And here I am.

She was about to put all her memories back in their place on the shelf, then realised she still had one album to look at, right at the bottom of the pile. What's this? I don't remember ever seeing this one. Alison tentatively opened up the first page. There was a pretty blonde lady, holding a baby, then another of a small baby naked in a bathtub, smiling up at the pretty lady holding a towel in her lap. There was a shot of a sandy beach, and a little girl playing in the waves, while the pretty lady looked on. Then a shot in a small room, cheaply furnished, with a nice looking man holding the little girl; next to him was an acoustic guitar resting on the couch. One on a swing, one playing on a slide, photo after photo of this little unit of people. Now why in God's name would her mother have these pictures... and why were they pasted in a book, in her closet at the bottom of the pile of family photos? Intriguing. Maybe these are old friends of hers or something, thought Alison. She flicked through page after page; finally getting to the end, nearly shutting the book, she noticed something bulky on the back cover lodged inside the plastic pocket.

She pulled it out, opened it up and began to read. It was a birth certificate. Alison Meredith Cunningham... Cunningham, thought Alison, what the hell? Born on November 15, 1950, time: 08:35, mother, Mary Cunningham, father David Cunningham. What is going on here, thought Alison? Oh my God, oh my God... and the proverbial penny had no choice but to drop. Oh my God, Mom and Dad Heart are not my real parents? Alice was shell shocked. Stunned, she sat there in a daze, trying to collect her thoughts.

So that's why I never felt the connection to them, she thought, that's it, I was not imagining it after all. So many pieces are falling into place now, so many things are finally making sense... And before she could completely digest this life changing revelation, she saw another slip of paper folded in the pocket.

Not knowing what to expect she extracted it from its resting place. It was an old newspaper article dated April 3, 1955. It was front page news, a horrific picture of a head on collision between a truck and a passenger car, the car obliterated, lying

on its side. She read below the picture: 'Accident...
On this unseasonably warm night, Mary and David
Cunningham, Cleveland Ohio, were out driving
home from Trude's Bar, where they worked as a
duo, with the top down. They had their daughter
with them. A long distance truck driver swerved
across the road, killing them both instantly, out on
I94 at midnight. There was one survivor in the car,
young Alison Meredith Cunningham, aged 4, who
was thrown out of the car on impact. She is in a
stable condition at St John's Hospital. In the other
vehicle was truck driver, Mr Lou Valensky of
Hamtramack, a suburb of Detroit. He escaped with
cuts and bruises and has now been arrested for
dangerous driving and may be charged with
manslaughter.'

This was a ridiculous amount of information
for any person to take in all at one time. Alice felt
like someone had punched her. She just sat there
swaying, head in her hands, putting it all together in
her mind.

Oh my God, she thought. The vision, the damn
vision, all my life, that pretty lady. It is real... I must
have been remembering my real mother all along.
Okay Mom Heart... can't wait for you to get back
and answer some serious questions. Funny though;
somewhere deep inside, she felt a calm coming over
her, a cold calm. She had always had a feeling that
something was not quite right at home. There were

always looks traded across the table between her parents whenever she did something unusual, always detours when she asked questions about being a baby, about her history, about when she was born... so many questions, and always smoke and mirrors. And that damn connection, no, she never felt it, even though she loved her mom and dad very much, it had to be said that they felt like emotional strangers, and now she knew why. But she needed to know why – why, why, why - why didn't anyone ever tell her? She had so many questions. She had no more time to waste, not one more minute of her life... Hurry Mom, get home.

On autopilot she got up from the table, carried the albums to her mother's bedroom and put them all back in their place, except the special one. She left it on the kitchen table waiting for her mom to return. She sat, drinking coffee, staring off into the distance, trying to assemble the chaos in her mind and heart. Okay, she thought, if I am adopted, which I obviously am, why wasn't I told? And why can't I remember things clearly? I know I was young, but surely I should have some kind of recollection. All I've ever had are these flashbacks, and I can never go deep into them. They come and go at will, never staying long enough for me to dive inside. Damn, I need some answers.

Then Mom Heart walked into the room.

Glancing down at the photo album, Mom Heart went white in the face and started to tremble.

"Oh Alison, what have you done? You were never supposed to see those pictures. I only put it with the rest of the albums because you don't live here anymore." She collapsed in the chair and began to cry. "I debated with my conscience so many times," she blurted out, knowing there was no point in lying about anything anymore. "Should I tell you, should I? I had always planned to, but the timing never seemed right," she sputtered and choked through her tears.

Alison didn't put her arm around her mom, she didn't do anything. She just sat there waiting for the explanation, waiting for the story that would make her life make emotional sense at last. Or so she hoped. From this point on, she was thinking, I am an island: nobody gets in and nobody gets out. The truth was, she was hurting.

Finally, Mom calmed down and began the story.

"Okay, here is exactly what happened. No more lies. As you see by the newspaper article, your parents were killed in a car crash. You survived, just. You were four years old. They put you into a coma for a few days to ease the pressure on your brain. When you awoke, you had no memory of anything. You didn't know your age, you didn't know even your name. At the hospital they showed you pictures of your mom and dad, and all you said was 'Who is pretty lady?' and 'Who is nice man?' You had no idea who they were, no idea that you were their child, no idea of anything. You were a blank canvass."

She continued slowly in a dull voice. "Your mom and dad were very poor. They had no surviving family, neither of them, which was unusual, and maybe why they were drawn together. You all lived in a very small apartment in a poor suburb. Because there was no family, once you were recovered sufficiently, they placed you in a children's home. Nobody came forward to claim you even after extensive news coverage. It was just heart-breaking. An orphan in the storm." Tears welled up in Mom Heart's eyes, but she willed them away and continued.

"So, there's your father and I, years and years married, but still no children, not his fault, my fault. They never knew the reason, I just never conceived. Eventually we decided we would adopt, a decision we took together right around the time of the accident. Since the story broke, I had been following it in the newspapers. I was heartbroken that a beautiful child like you (the news printed your picture) should be in an orphanage, so I made the necessary steps to see if we could possibly foster you. It took about nine months but then we were successful and finally able to take you home. You were very withdrawn, very quiet, hardly spoke a word. I felt from the first time I read about the accident that I was connected to you somehow... don't ask me why, I have no idea. I had numerous meetings during the first year with the doctor who treated you after the accident. They told me that you will probably never remember anything of the early years of your life. That you had suffered a great shock when you were thrown from the car and your brain was traumatised and erased by the crash, totally. So, your dad and I made the decision to keep a photo album, with everything we could gather, so that someday, when we felt the time was right, we could present it to you, and you would know who you were. You deserved to know who you were. But that time never came... and then you left home... and then you became famous. I figured it was maybe for the best that you never did know. I figured it was best to just sweep it all under the carpet. But now it seems fate has stepped in and you discovered the truth. I know you must be angry. I know you must be confused, Alison; my intention was never to hurt you or to lie to you. I loved you like my own. Dad does too. You were always my child.... my child, but, as you now know, you are not my child."

Silence.

Alison got up from the chair, very quietly, very deliberately. "I'm going for a walk around the old neighbourhood. I need to be alone."

Ambling aimlessly along the familiar streets, she walked and thought, walked and thought, through a maze of confusion and questions.

Boy, I always wondered who in the family I looked like. I could never see any of either of my parents in my face, my body, my mannerisms... nothing. Even when I met Mom's sister, Aunt Lisa, and my first cousin Benjamin, nothing, zilch. I was completely different. Now it makes sense. I do not belong to them. From what I saw in the pictures, even just looking at them the one time, I take after my mother in looks, but with my father's build. What were they like, I wonder? Were they smart, were they kind, were they talented, did either of them sing or play an instrument? What job did my father do for a living? Was my mother happy? And most importantly, where are they buried? Then, maybe I can fill in these empty emotional spaces, spaces that have always been there. Maybe I can make sense of my flashbacks, maybe I can actually remember... that would be great. I am on a quest from this moment on. I want to know everything there is to know.

And her search began, and for the next few days she went here and there and everywhere, searching for clues, going to the library, looking at newspaper articles, searching for anyone who might have known them. She let Harry and Oliver know that she would be staying in Cleveland for a little longer, telling them she had "family duty calls." Finally, Alison got lucky. There was one name mentioned, a woman who had come forward to say that she knew the Cunninghams very well since they lived in the same apartment block, and that she used to go and watch them perform. More than once she had babysat the little Alison while her parents did their thing. Her name was Daniella O'Donnel. Alice found herself at her apartment, ringing the bell, the very next day.

Daniella opened the door.

"Yes, can I help you my dear?" Then she had a shock as she realised this was Alison Heart standing in front of her: Cleveland's own famous rock chick. What the hell was she doing on her doorstep? There was something in the way this young woman stood there, her stance, her attitude, something so familiar to Daniella and yet...? Alison came straight to the point.

"Hello Daniella, if I may call you by your first name. I hope I haven't put you into a shock. Yes, I am Alison Heart. I have tracked you down because I understand you were friends with Mary and David Cunningham. And I have just found out that they were my real parents. May I come in?"

Sitting on the faded sofa in the tiny living room, Daniella began the story Alison was so desperate to hear.

Chapter Nineteen

Mary and David Cunningham

Mary Cunningham, nee Branston, was born February 8th 1914 in Baton Rouge to a poor farming family. She was an only child born unexpectedly to elderly parents, Gwenda and Peter Branston. Although there were farm hands to help out around the place, Mary grew up lonely having no sisters or brothers to play with. She was a beautiful but quiet child, living inside of her imagination most of the time, as only children tend to do. Her favourite thing as she was growing up was to sing along to recordings of the popular singers of the day, pretending she was on the stage. She had a good voice, and even as a child and could imitate just about anyone. The strangest thing was, though, she preferred to sing the male songs. These resonated with her better than the female ones. But it was all daydreams. Yes, she could sing, but what hope could there possibly be for a poor farmer's daughter from a small town with no prospects of bettering her life? "Well, I can dream can't I?" she said, and that is what she did.

Mary's father Peter passed away when she was 18 years old from an unexpected bad heart. It was a shock because he seemed to be such a robust strong man. Her mother followed soon after, a victim of stomach cancer. So from an only child she became an orphan. Mary took the money from the sale of the farm and relocated to Nashville, and got a job as a waitress in a bar in the main street of town. It was not the most exciting job in the world, but at least there was a life here to be lived. And there was music everywhere, heaven! Mary worked and dreamed her dreams of being a singer, day after day. And then she met David.

David Cunningham was born on March 3rd 1913 to a poor mining family in the South Dakota Hills. He, too, was an only child, born late in life for Susan Cunningham, who was 45 years old. Both she and her husband, Jimmy Cunningham, had given up on ever having kids. David was a loner, both in himself and also out of necessity, having no siblings to play with. Mining families were notorious for keeping themselves to themselves. And to make things more difficult, Jimmy up and left them in the middle of the night. There was no reason, he just went. Poor Susan's heart was broken. She held on to her son as if her very life depended on it, making them unnaturally close. She never had another man in her life, or at least no-one David was aware of.

David led a very solitary lonely life, confused about having to be the man of the family, yet still being a child. He loved his mother very much and vowed to always protect her. He also promised himself that one day he would track down his father and find out why he left. David was the kind of person who kept his promises, especially to himself. He loved his father but it was tinged with a deep seated anger. He accepted he was an only child, but he did not accept he was fatherless when he knew his father was alive and well. Something told him this was so, and he would one day find him.

One love he found very early on, around age 8, was the guitar. This interest came through listening to country music played on the radio. He and his mother listened out on the porch of their shack in the early evening. He fell in love with the stories the singers told and decided he would play acoustic guitar. Saving up all his pocket money, and with a little help from his mother on the quiet, he was finally able to purchase a cheap folk guitar. From that moment on, he had a true friend, his music. He even started to compose songs, and discovered he had a talent. He knew his voice was just average, but he got away with it, especially singing self-composed tunes. The emotion carried him through.

David started to work in some bars around town, just him, his guitar and his music. He earned an okay living. It was enough to save a little, so that he could realise his dream of getting out of South Dakota, and going somewhere bigger and better, where music was important. One day, mind made up, he went to his mother and explained his non-negotiable decision. He would always remember her sitting on her little rocking chair on the porch as he told her. She was crying her eyes out, yet at the same time telling him he had to go and follow his dream. This was the last memory he had of his mother. He was never to see her alive again. She died of a heart attack, one year later. The authorities tracked David down to a bar in Nashville where he was singing four sets a night and told him the news. David went back home, tied up all the loose ends on the property, took what little money that brought, buried his mother, and said goodbye to his past. He was now the 'lone wolf' that he had always felt like. Then came Mary.

As fate would have it, both Mary and David were now in Nashville, the music capital of America, although they did not know each other yet. David had a residency on the main street in a funky bar called Randy's Place, playing four sets a night. He did a combination of covers and originals, and had a steady appreciative audience. One night, mid-week, Mary decided to tool on down to the bar and listen for herself. Friends of hers at work had told her about this interesting guitarist, singer, songwriter and she was curious. For some unknown reason she made an effort that night, dressing in her sexiest tight blue jeans and soft white blouse with her long brown hair hanging loose down her back. Blue cowboy boots completed the look. She walked into the bar at 9pm. It wasn't real busy just yet; the bulk of the usual crowd arrived around 10. She took a seat at the bar, near the stage, ordered a beer and turned towards the stage on her stool, as David Cunningham entered to begin the night's entertainment. It was immediate lust at first sight, for both of them. They locked eyes somewhere in the middle of the first song he sang, ironically one he had written called 'Where Did You Come From?' The chorus went:

> 'Where did you come from?
> Where are you going?
> Where did you come from?
> You get my juices going.
> Where did you come from?
> Know that we're knowing
> Where we are going.'

David finished his first set, and casually made his way to the stool next to Mary. He ordered a shot of whiskey. Neither of them spoke for a few seconds, then they both spoke at once. It took no time at all to establish the attraction, introduce themselves, and do the blah blah blah, ending in David asking for Mary's telephone number. He called the next day, and arranged to take her out to dinner on his night off which was Sunday. They met, they talked, they drank, they ate, then they went home to his apartment and made love all night long. From that moment on they were a couple.

Mary and David settled into a nice routine and found that they were very compatible. Mary continued waitressing and David continued his residency at Randy's Place. Then, one lazy Sunday, the strangest thing happened. David was working on a new song he wanted to try. Mary had been listening for about a week now as he fiddled around with it trying to get the music and lyrics to gel. Without thinking, Mary started to sing the song. It was a hauntingly beautiful bluesy number.

David kept playing, and listened closely.

'Baby baby baby,
Whatcha you doin' to me
You done stole my heart
Put these chains on me
Will I ever be free, will I ever be free
Baby baby baby
Whatcha done to me.'

My God, he thought. She really interprets my song perfectly. My God indeed. Mary should be singing with me on stage. He put down his guitar, ran into the other room, grabbed her by the waist, threw her onto the bed and said, "You are my new singer. You are going to quit your job and we are going to work at Randy's as a duo. How does that grab you?"

"Oh David, you have no idea. I have wanted to sing my whole life. And I love your originals. I also love the covers you do, they suit me. Do you really think I am good enough to do this on stage? I won't make a fool of myself will I?"

"Nope, you won't. It's a done deal." Mary and David became a team, onstage and off. They were happy with their lot.

At some point they decided to move to another city. Nashville had become a little predictable and they thought a change might do some good. Throwing ideas back and forth, they settled on Cleveland Ohio, for no reason in particular. They both just liked the sound of it. David did some research into live music venues. There seemed to be a lot of the 'live' bars that he usually played. He made a few calls, and secured enough gigs to make the journey worthwhile. They didn't need much, either of them, both being from poor beginnings. All they really needed was each other. They found a nice clean but cheap apartment that they could afford. The bonus was their next door neighbour Daniella O'Donnel who Mary quickly became best friends with, like the sister she never had. They shared life stories early on, and were inseparable.

Then Mary fell pregnant. David was over the moon about it, even though they really couldn't manage another mouth to feed. They would find a way.

So, Mary and David Cunningham became Mary, David and Alison Meredith Cunningham. They spent their weeks going from bar to bar, playing their music. There was always somebody to look after the baby while they were onstage. David had bought a very old Chevy convertible, just big enough for his guitar, amp, and the baby cot in the back.

Chapter Twenty

Then, That Night

On April 3, 1955, there was the car crash, the death of her parents, and everything changed for little Alison Meredith Cunningham, although she would have no recollection of this part of her life. The cards had been dealt.

Alison sat still and quietly, with a strong shot of whiskey, trying to digest the entire story. Daniella had said that she was her mother 's best friend and there was no doubt in her mind that every detail was true. It felt true, it rang true, it was true; it was her history, before she became Alison Meredith Heart, before she became the famous rock chick/guitarist Alison Heart.

"I have some old photos of my mother and father that Mom Heart kept in a book for me. Do you have anything to add to my collection? I would like everything possible to try and put my life together. I so appreciate you sharing this with me, you have no idea. The shock when I found out. To find out that I am not who I thought I was. You can imagine. And, because I am now famous, I would not like the press to get hold of this. I would appreciate it if you kept this to yourself. You were my Mom's best friend, and if she trusted you, so shall I. I am not sure if I want the world to know about this yet, not sure at all. So please respect my decision. I need time to deal with this and digest it properly."

She knew she was talking a blue streak but she had to get it all out.

"I need to know so much Daniella. What was I like as a child? Quiet, talkative, shy, precocious, smart, clingy? Did my mother kiss me a lot, or was I a Daddy's girl? Was I loved?" Then she stopped, realising that this was the most important question of all. And she was more than a little embarrassed that she had asked it. She had exposed her mojo.

Daniella looked long and hard at Alison, and then said, "First I'm going to refill your whiskey glass, then get some pictures for you to look at, and I will answer all your questions the best I can." Alison sat quietly sipping her whiskey.

Daniella came back with a stack of loose photos. "I am not a paste the picture in a book type of person... so, Alison, here we go." She flipped from one faded wrinkled picture to the next.

"This is your mom and dad about three weeks after you were born. See how happy and proud they look. That's you in the cot covered by a blanket. Now here's a picture of all of us on the way to one of the bars they played at. I was to babysit for the night. That's you in the child seat... you're about three years old here. See how pretty you are. You were always smiling. You were a very happy baby, a very happy child, very wanted and loved. In fact, the three of you were the perfect unit.

"Oh, I love this next one... this is you and your dad. See how he is looking at you, so protective. I always remember him saying that you had changed his life, that you did things to him deep inside. You touched him where nobody else had ever touched. He didn't think it was possible to love anyone so much. Your dad was a very nice man, but a little aloof... not snobby aloof just... mmm, I don't know, hard to get in to. He kept himself to himself. But you, oh my God, he loved you so much. He loved your mother too but I have to say, if I am being honest, he loved you more. You were his life.

"And here is your mother... aw, God I just loved your mother. She was a genuinely kind caring person. My best friend Mary. I never had a friend like her in my whole life. We were more like sisters really. She never wanted anything from anyone, always accepted whatever life threw at her, and just got on with it. She loved you unconditionally, she loved your father the same way. Mary was an all or nothing person. When she loved she loved without end. I was lucky to have her as a friend."

Alison took a deep breath; she had one last question.

"Where are they buried?" she said quietly. Daniella replied, "At the cemetery on the corner of Douglas and Fairbanks. They are buried side by side, right next to the gardener's shed in the north corner just off the walking path. I have been there many times myself."

"I don't believe it Daniella, that's the exact place my friends and I used to hang out when we were teenagers, drinking beer and smoking... Oh my God, I may have walked over their grave many times and never known it. Wow!"

And finally, it was evening, and the conversation came to a natural end.

"Well, Alison, that's it, that's the whole story, I have no more to say, no more pictures to show you, no more light to shine on your past. I hope I have been of some help. When they died I never quite came to terms with it. I wanted to help out somehow, but didn't know what to do. I am alone, no husband, so adoption agencies would not be so quick to let me have you. And, anyway, I am not sure that's what your parents would have wanted. I was so confused, so sad, so angry at what happened. After the initial news coverage I simply withdrew from the whole scenario. I never stopped wondering what happened to you, and now, here you are."

They both sat quietly, immersed in their private thoughts, then they hugged long and hard.

"Thank you Daniella, honestly, thank you so much. I am sorry for just turning up like this. But, once I discovered my truth, I had to track you down. Thank God you are still here and were able to fill in the missing pieces. I think my real mother and father would be happy that we have talked. And I know in my heart that they are so happy to finally be remembered. I now, thanks to you, have my roots firmly in place. I know who I am, I know where I came from, and I know that I was very loved. Thank you thank you thank you. I will keep in touch if that's okay." Alison rose from the couch, kissed Daniella on the cheek, and left, lost in her swirling emotions. She felt like she had been blown over by a hurricane. This had been one hell of a trip home.

Alison got into her parents' old Chevy wagon. She knew exactly where to go: the graveyard. Parking the car on the side street she strode purposefully in, walking quickly down the path and turning left to the spot Daniella described. As she neared the gardener's shed, she slowed down, wanting to see the tombstone, yet not wanting to see it. And there it was. Jesus Christ. A downmarket tombstone marked the spot. Nothing special, just the names.

David 1913-1955 and Mary Cunningham 1914 -1955, R.I.P. She dropped to her knees, grabbed the stone, and cried like a baby. She cried for the lost baby/child that would maybe never remember her beginnings. She cried for the emotionally confused girl growing up, and she cried for her broken heart that was an essential part of the woman she now was. She cried until she stopped.

Now that she had filled in the missing pieces of her life, decisions needed to be made. How would she handle Mom and Dad Heart? They were not evil people. They loved her and had given her much love, a nice home, a safe world to grow up in. Hurting them was not an option. I guess I will have to tackle this head on, with both of them, she thought. Be honest, explain how I feel, and tell them that I don't blame them for anything. They did what they thought was best at the time. I will not hurt them. I love them both.

Continuing down her 'things to deal with' list... Harry, oh my God, Harry, my husband. What do I do about him? I always counted on him being in my life, my lover, my best friend, my man. Oh boy, now the goal posts have moved, and I have no idea how I am going to handle this. It's hard enough trying to come to terms with the fact that I've just had my first affair, and, to make it worse, I think I am in love with the guy. Now what? Should I meet Leo in Miami and make things even more difficult?

Should I not go and deny myself the most deliciously abandoned feelings I have ever experienced in my life? Whatever this is, I'm sure it doesn't come knocking twice. Shit, shit, shit... One door closes, another one opens. I have got some serious thinking to do.

And what better place to do it than in her old bedroom, in Cleveland Ohio, with Mom and Dad Heart. Alison made her way back to her childhood home to face her demons.

She pulled up slowly into the driveway, got out, locked the door, and let herself in the back door. Her mom and dad were waiting for her, sitting at the kitchen table, both with a glass of wine, which was unusual, as they normally didn't drink. I guess they need fortification tonight, she thought. She pulled up a chair, got a glass, poured herself a drink, and began to talk.

"Mom... Dad... don't say anything... let me get this all out in one go. So, as you now know Dad, I found the photo album, and Mom has told me the whole story. For the last couple of days I have been researching into the lives of my real mother and father. I was able to track down Mom's best friend here Daniella O'Donnel, and she filled me in with the rest of the story, right up until the crash... the rest, as they say, is history.

"I want to be completely honest with you because this is the only way forward. I love you both dearly but, as I am sure you have realised through the years, I have never felt the deep 'daughter' connection with you. I was always aware of the silent messages passing between you when I asked too many questions, or when I acted strangely. I am sure you were both thinking 'Well, she is not really our daughter.' Which was the truth.

"I have been searching my whole life for a clue to why I have always felt like an orphan - there was no reason. I had a mom and dad, I had a home, a life, but I just did not fit in. Guess it is in the blood after all. I don't blame you. I thank God that you took me in. You are good people and you have given me a good life. I will always love you and be grateful for that. But now, I must put the pieces of my early years together and let it see where it leads me. I have been to the graveyard and made my peace, but my heart is hungry, my soul is hungry. I want... I want the whole truth and nothing less will do.

"Mom, at this stage I don't have anything more to add about the other situation; sorry Dad, but this is between us. I will keep you informed Mom, whatever happens. Nothing will be 'overnight'. I am not a foolish person. I am going to call Oliver and ask him to book me on the next flight back to London. And now I need to go to bed. I am physically and emotionally exhausted. I love you both... goodnight."

The Hurricane

Not one more word in this house... not a creature was stirring, not even a mouse.

The next morning, Alison's parents drove her to the airport. She flew to New York, and spent the night at the Warwick in order to catch her direct flight back to London the next day. The Warwick: the hotel where everything changed for her. What a greenhorn in love she was, and didn't even know it. She was starving and didn't even know it. Oh boy oh boy oh boy.

Checking in, she went directly to her room, the Cary Grant suite of course. I wonder if he had any problems like this, she thought. Sure, he must have, he was a big movie star of the day, and being famous never comes without its full quota of problems, professional and personal, but mostly personal. It sure does change the game plan. Everything is there for the taking, yet there is always the danger of the 'public' to deal with. Nothing is private anymore. A secret affair, ha... sure, it's private at the moment but for how long? Only until a paparazzi gets hold of it. Same as the story of my real parents... boy, what a field day they would have... it would sell newspapers for weeks. I am going to keep both things close to my chest.

Leo and I are so damn well-known. How can this possibly go anywhere without destroying everything in its path? Guilt was now making an appearance in Alison's mind, resting in her heart.

Oh Harry, she thought, you don't deserve this. You have done nothing but love me from day one. God, who needs these thoughts or these problems?

The entire evening stretched in front of her. There was one call she knew she had to make. She had promised Leo she would call before she left for London and let him know her decision about Miami, although it was a decision she had not yet made. She dialled the private number tentatively. Leo answered on the first ring.

"Hello my sweetness. I have been waiting for your call. I thought maybe you had deserted me. I have not stopped thinking about you. I can still feel you, I can still taste you. You have invaded my life... hello... are you there?"

Pause.

"Hello Leo. Sorry I didn't call earlier. I had to take an unexpected trip to Cleveland and visit my parents. I fly back to London tomorrow morning. I had a lot of unexpected personal issues to deal with... you are one of them."

Pause.

"Our night together was the most magical of my entire life, and I do not say that lightly. To be honest, this kind of intensity scares the shit out of me. I have never never loved like this before. Do I want this, do I need this... Do you?"

Pause.

"Well, I don't have the answer to this question my sweetness. My position is even more precarious than yours. I am an older man, with an established marriage, kids, grandchildren... my entire image is based on this. The Kings, one of show business' strongest marriages. My God, the articles and home stories we have done celebrating our relationship. And now... and now..." Leo stuttered. "And now... what the hell should we do?"

Pause.

"Let's talk about Miami," Alison blurted out. "When is it exactly? When do you need my decision? How long would I be staying? How the hell can we get away with this? We are both public personas so easily recognised. Jesus, is this even a good idea?"

Pause.

"The trip is planned now for about six weeks' time. I am staying in a private apartment on Fisher Island. We will be secluded and protected. I don't need anyone to get wind of this any more than you do. Please come Alison. At least we can spend the week together and see if we have a future, or if it is simply chemistry rearing its head. Although I think I do know which it is. Say you'll come... unless we give this a go I will never know a moment's peace, and I am pretty long in the tooth to be going through that scenario."

Pause.

There was a tug of war between her head and her heart... heart won.

"Okay Leo. I will come. Give me all the necessary details and I will have my record company book it up. I need to create a lie for Harry, and for Oliver too, although he will guess for sure, he is one smart cookie, and he knows me inside and out. As for Harry, he will believe what I tell him, without question... not a good beginning, is it Leo, lies?"

Pause.

"Anyway, that's not your problem, that's mine. I am sure you have your own to sort out."

Pause.

Oh yes, thought Leo. Malinda wants to come with me and make it a second honeymoon. Oh, what are we doing to each other? But I am in too deep to walk away.

Pause.

"Okay then Alison, I will get you the details and you make your arrangements. Is there a private number I can call you on?"

"You'd better go through the record company. You have that number. And we'd better have a code name too. Let's see, what can we call us? Okay, I've got it. The codeword is The Hurricane... let's hope we both don't blow it. Sorry, that's my black sense of humour making an appearance. Leave that name and I will call you back on this number. Gotta go to bed now Leo, my flight is early tomorrow morning. Anon."

There was a long pause, with breathing heavy on both ends.

Alison hung up first.

What the hell am I doing? thought Alison.

What the hell am I doing? pondered Leo, and hung up.

The flight back was too short for her to sleep properly, but at least it was nice and smooth. Alison was not a good flyer. Harry would be at the airport to meet her and she was not looking forward to it, simply because she was a shitty liar. Well, it was time to use the best of her acting abilities. No way could Harry even suspect something, at least not until after the trip, so she could see which way the wind was blowing. And, after 'the hurricane', who knew who would still be standing?

Dark glasses on, short fur jacket, skin tight black jeans, high heels, rolling Louis Vuitton bag, looking every inch a star, Alison got off the plane where she was met by the vip people and whisked through security, her bags collected, and escorted to Harry who was waiting in a special room for her. Ah, the perks of being famous. Right, she thought, here we go.

"Hi honey. So good to see you. I missed you," said Alice, but wisely kept her sunglasses on; windows of the soul and all that, she thought. She gave him a big hug, and avoided the kiss on the lips. The hug felt good, as it always did. My Harry... boy, this is not going to be easy. She was back home, and with quite a lot of excess baggage of the emotional kind, although Harry had no idea. Bless him, she thought, he is so trusting. Then a song came to mind... All my love all my kissin', you don't know what you've been a missing oh boy... oh boy is right!

Alison had been home about a week when the wave of inspiration came. She started to write songs, one after the other, Leo King being her inspiration. They were songs unlike anything she had written before, with a depth, with heartache, with confusion, laced with wisdom. She had never been so creative. Each new song she played to Harry, who listened attentively, but, it must be said, looked confused. He finally asked, "Where are these songs coming from darling, especially these lyrics - they are excellent but wow, what's happened to you?"

"Oh, I guess I am simply growing up, exploring my heart a little deeper, you know, letting the woman out, going the distance, questioning things, giving my artistic self-licence to fly. Don't know Harry... but while this inspiration is here, I am going to keep writing until it stops." And then, in their home studio, she said: "Here, help me put some of these down on the cassette machine so I can play them to Oliver." And they worked as a team like they always had done. Alice, on piano, put down the opening strains of a new song:

> 'Blue jeaned dreams, on satin pillows
> Tears of regret, rip me apart
> Childish poems, like weeping willows
> Tear the roots right from my heart
> Crazy night of mixed emotions
> Whisper secrets, to the night
> Shall I whisper my devotion
> And then put my wings in flight'

Alison's arms came up in goose bumps as she sang. Mmmm, the notes of my destiny... Harry got goose bumps too. Mmmm, the notes of my fate... And they worked on through the night together.

Oh what tangled webs we weave, when we practice to deceive, said the spider to the fly.

After a couple of weeks at home, and one unavoidable time in bed, where for the first time in their relationship Alison had to fake it, she told Harry: "I'm going to go in and see Oliver, honey. No need to come. Just want to sort out a few bits and pieces, maybe book some studio time. We've been working hard on these new songs for a few days now, why don't you have some down time? Go and please yourself, go shooting or something."

Harry agreed; the deck was clear. She now needed to make some concrete arrangements, in person, not over the phone. Alison dressed carefully in her best 'star, casual' clothes, called a taxi and made her way to the record company office for her 1pm meeting with Oliver.

Oliver stood up, quickly walked over to Alison and gave her a big friendly paternal hug. He was genuinely fond of her. "So, my wandering rock star, it's good to see you. I understand from Harry that you have been writing up a storm, and that the stuff is g.o.o.d. About time too: your next album is due out in eight months and we need to go in and start recording as soon as possible."

"I know Oliver, that's why I am here. I've brought in a few rough demos of the new stuff for you to listen to. It's a totally new approach, not so much Alison but a lot more Heart. I want to make this album my coming of age, my Tapestry, if you like. Also, I do need to make that trip to Miami next month, and I need to go alone. I am on a roll with these songs and I need some space, peace and quiet away from everyone including Harry. I want to stay for a week. Can you clear this with my husband, so it's on your orders, make him busy here on something? He can do the pre work at the studio, hire the musicians, get the top lines done etc etc... just make it non-negotiable. I need to make this trip. I will make my own accommodation arrangements. I guess you can say I am doing late night talk shows or something... just find an excuse. Please."

Hmm, thought Oliver, something is up here, and it's something serious. My guess is she has met someone, someone who could be life changing... it all makes sense, the cloak and dagger routine, the songs, the trip. Oh well, I knew eventually this would happen. Still, it's sad. I do like good old Harry, he is a nice, real person. In fact his only downfall really is his inability to change. He simply is who he is. Aloud he said, "Okay, no problem. I will take care of everything this end. I will listen to the new stuff this evening and give you my thoughts on it. Sounds like you're on a roll Alison, maybe not a rock and roll, but definitely a roll." Oliver laughed aloud, loving his quick wit. Alison tried to laugh with him. "How about we call the album 'The Heart Of Alison'?"

"Done deal, I like it... and Oliver, thank you."

At home Alison made a cup of coffee in her huge country kitchen, a respite as Harry was out shooting. She was sitting there staring into space when the phone rang. It was her record company, Crown Records. Nose up her own backside Angela, Oliver's assistant, announced primly, "Hello Ms Heart, we have made your arrangements. First class to Miami, July 24th, returning August 1st, and here's the flight number. Also, somebody left a strange message on the answer phone. Said could you call him at home, and his name was The Hurricane?"

"Thank you Angela. Please make sure the tickets are sent to me at home. I will also need a limo to and from the airport. Can you also make sure I have the first row aisle seat both ways? Is Oliver there? I need a quick word."

"I'll put you right through."

"Yes, Alison? What can I do for you? Did Angela give you all the information?"

"Yep, got it. Thanks. Can you please clear the deck with Harry as soon as possible? I don't want to tell him about my trip until after you have told him that you need him to be around to help out with arrangements for the recording. Once you have done that, I will explain how I need some space to finish my writing. Tomorrow would be good."

"Done and dusted my little rock star..." They both hung up.

Next Alison dialled Leo's private number.

"Hello Leo, it's me, Alison. How are you?"

"Ah, wonderful to hear your voice my sweetness. I have been waiting for you to call me, and now here you are. Have you made your arrangements?"

"It's good to hear your voice too Leo. You have been on my mind more than is comfortable... and yes, I have made my arrangements. I will arrive on British Airways in Miami on July 24th at 14:30, and will leave on Aug 1st at 22:00. I will be bringing my acoustic guitar with me. I have some new songs to finish, and I don't suppose there's any chance that there will be a piano in the apartment?"

"Probably not my sweetness, but whatever you want you shall have. I will make sure there is one, and if possible in a private room so you can have some privacy. I understand it is quite a large luxurious apartment. So, you're writing some new songs... interesting, I assume for your new album. Tell me, are any of them about me?"

Long pause.

"Only all of them Leo. If you are a good boy I may play you a few. You have thrown me in a completely new direction. This 'whatever it is' between us has unleashed the woman in me big time. And I must give her her voice. Boy, my fans are going to be shocked. I'm shocked, my husband is totally confused, my record company boss knows something is going on. I just don't know what's happening to me." The next thought she kept to herself: but I have decided to ride this ride to the end.

Harry was out early the next morning for his meeting with Oliver. Alison was still sleeping so he left her in peace, leaving her a note. When he got home later that afternoon he had some questions to ask.

Alison was sitting on the couch watching her favourite afternoon game shows; she was addicted to quizzes.

"Oh hi honey, how did the meet go?"

"Fine; Oliver has given me loads of things to set up for the recording... which is being scheduled when you return from Miami. I repeat: when you return from Miami? What's going on Alison? You've never needed space from me to get your song-writing done. Why now? Have I done something wrong? Are we okay? I am floundering here and feeling more than a little insecure. I think it's time we had a little talk darlin', don't you?"

Alison patted the seat next to her on the couch. "Sit down Harry, take a load off." She was playing it as cool and casual as she could. "Nothing is wrong honey. I am in this weird creative phase and want to explore it. I want to be completely alone. I need to be completely alone. It's only for a week. You will be busy anyway. No big deal."

There was no reason to destroy this man's life until she was sure that it needed to happen, and at this moment in time she wasn't sure of anything, only that she had to meet Leo and see where destiny would take her. 'She's gotta ticket to ride'... don't you just love the Beatles?

She gave Harry a peck on the cheek and laid her head on his shoulder, snuggling up close. Mmm, she thought, this does feel comfortable. He is a good man, and I do love him, but God help me, I am not 'in love' anymore. This is a fact. Leo or no Leo. Something has died. Bless you Harry, you did nothing to deserve this. Alison fleetingly considered telling Harry about her discovery in Cleveland, but didn't. It was strange, she thought, considering how close they were... but there, that's the clue: how close they 'were', not 'are'. They both watched the quiz show.

The next couple of weeks passed quickly, too quickly for Harry's liking. He had a sense of doom about this trip his wife was taking. Pottering around the kitchen, Harry said out loud, without realising it: "She is so distant lately, we're just not connecting like we used to. Can't put my finger on it, but it's there. Damn, what the hell is going on?" The million dollar question, he thought, what the hell indeed.

Finally it was July 23rd, the night before the trip. Alison was packed and ready to go, more than ready. She had taken very few clothes: one tight figure hugging black dress, nylons and high heeled shoes, in case they went out for dinner; one track suit, pink of course with matching trainers; one pair of cut-off Levi's, four t-shirts, and her airplane outfit. She guessed she wouldn't need any nightwear... or hopefully not anyway. Her guitar, song-writing pad and pen and little recorder sat next to her small double decker rolling Louise Vuitton suitcase. She would insist that they allow her to take on her guitar too; after all, it was first class. There would be no waiting for baggage, just as she liked it, being impatient with a capital I.

The Hurricane

She had first planned her airplane outfit; this always came before anything else, and she would always wear it to and from wherever she was going. Everything else would fit around this. She chose light coloured blue jeans, a very thin light leather jacket with a white silk scarf to protect her throat (air conditioning on the plane could be brutal), a white t-shirt, and white cowboy boots, topped off with a large pair of white Cartier sunglasses. A fleeting thought crossed her mind... Hmm, I am due on this week, which is a complete drag, but funny, I don't feel like my period is coming at all... strange, I guess it's just nerves. Well, can't be helped, we will just have to deal with it when it does arrive. Finally it was bedtime. Alison knew what was coming and was prepared.

Harry climbed into bed, strangely silent for once, and began to make love to her; not love with her, love to her... she knew it, he knew it.

Chapter Twenty-One

July 24 1978 Miami

A limo met Alison at the airport and she gave the driver the address. Leo was already there. It was a normal blistering hot sunny day. "Please turn off the air conditioning, I want to put the windows down. Off I go... Follow the yellow brick road," she sang to herself, daydreaming happily along the route until finally a sign read Fisher Island, and as they pulled up to a sumptuous, obviously wealthy apartment block, Alison thought: now I know I'm not in Kansas anymore. The driver unloaded her cases and carried them to the door, waiting to be let in. Of course, Alison didn't want any nosey parkers having any information; after all she was Alison Heart, instantly recognisable, and Leo was an instantly recognisable television talk show host. "Thank you very much, I can handle everything from here on in." She gave him a tip, and dismissed him. Then she took a very big deep breath and rang the doorbell.

Leo opened the door immediately, took one look at Alison standing there with her little case and guitar, looking strangely vulnerable for a famous rock chick, pulled her cases inside, shut the door and let loose. The passion was electric as they ripped each other's clothes off, spreading them in a heap all over the tiled floored in the foyer. No bedroom was necessary; they simply fell to the ground and got reacquainted. It was over quickly, and neither of them minded.

Alison broke the silence first. "Well, that's what I call a hello!"

Much later, after a slow leisurely second round of mind blowing sex - much slower mind blowing sex - they slept, arms and legs intertwined as if their bodies were made for each other... and maybe they were. Time would tell.

Leo woke first, not knowing for a moment where he was or indeed who he was lying next to. Then, remembering every delicious detail, he carefully rolled on his side and gazed down at the 'famous rock chick' lying in his bed, looking nothing like a famous rock chick. Her hair was spread over the pillow, one arm up under her head, one arm down, in a semi foetal position, which looked very erotic to him... sexy is in the eyes of the beholder, indeed. He lay there and stared, drinking her in. Never did he think this could happen to him, not at his age, my God pushing 60!... and having an affair with Alison Heart. And twice in one night... Leo, he thought to himself, when you fall off the wagon you fall off real good don't you... and then, finally, Alison opened her eyes.

They stared deep into each other's souls, united in the cosmos, non-negotiably 'in love' and not a damn thing either of them could do about it.

"Good morning Leo." She stretched her body up sleepily. "Mmm... what did you do to me last night, you dirty old man... and whatever is was, can I have some more please?"

And so their day began.

Much later, Leo went out attending to some business in downtown Miami, leaving Alison with her thoughts. She sat in the kitchen, her favourite place no matter where she was, casual in her pink track suit and bare feet, hair loose and hanging down with that undeniable glow to her cheeks, the glow of a woman who has spent the night and the morning making love. She looked at the calendar on the wall: July 25th. "I've been here one day already," she spoke out loud, "Six more to go."

Wait a minute, she thought... July 25th. Wait a minute.

I'm not due on this week, I was due on last week, and I am never ever late. As a matter of fact, I didn't get my period the month before either, but with all the travelling and emotional upset, I just didn't think about it... Oh no, Jesus Christ, don't tell me, no it can't be, I can't be pregnant. I just can't be, but I could be... of course it could be Harry's... but I don't think so. Shit.

Alison realised that she had been feeling tired lately, not herself, out of sorts, and had put it down to the stress of the situation she was in, never thinking for a minute that on that one night in New York this could have happened, not this. She called a cab and asked to be taken to the nearest drug store, where she bought two pregnancy testing kits, and went back to the apartment, straight to the toilet, hoping that she was wrong... of course she wasn't. She was pregnant. She sat down on the couch, poured herself a stiff Jack Daniels, and awaited Leo's return.

He arrived around 6pm, with a huge bouquet of flowers and a bottle of Cristal Champagne. Looking glorious in his business suit, all classy and elegant, he strode purposefully into the room. He looked at his Alice, sitting on the couch, deposited the flowers and champagne on the hall table, and dropped to his knees. "Let's celebrate tonight. We have found each other my sweetness, and you have given me feelings I never thought I would have, not in this lifetime anyway. Dare I say it... I love you."

He kissed her softly and romantically, not wanting this moment to turn into sex. It was a tender heartfelt moment and he wanted to keep it on that level. Leo, normally a guarded man, was completely exposed, naked, unsure, happy, sad, confused; in fact the only thing he was sure of was that he was indeed in love, maybe for the first time in his life. Alison kissed him back just as tenderly; they were on the same page.

As he broke the embrace, he noticed the testing kits lying on the coffee table. It didn't register for a few seconds, and then it did. "Alison... don't tell me... are you... are you pregnant?"

"Yes Leo, I am pregnant. I am pretty damn sure it is yours, as the dates work out perfect. Of course I have not been to the doctor yet, I only realised it as I was sitting in the kitchen this morning, that I was late. Late by two months going on three!"

It was hard to gauge Leo's reaction. Shocked was an appropriate word for both of them. He rose off his knees, and walked very slowly over to the hall table, giving himself time to think. He brought over the flowers, gave them to Alison, walked over to the small kitchen, grabbed two champagne glasses and an ice bucket, popped the cork, walked back to the couch, still in slow motion, poured the champagne, giving one to Alison, and then, finally, a smile appeared. "To us my sweetness, and to whoever is growing inside of your beautiful tummy. It looks like fate has taken any hesitation out of the equation. We belong together. I do love you." They clinked glasses, the deal was done. Lives were about to be destroyed.

The next few days passed in a whirlwind of love making and discussions. After the shock had worn off, they began to talk about their future. There were so many problems ahead: Leo's wife Malinda, Leo's children and grandchildren, Alison's husband Harry. How was it going to work? The media... the problems were huge in every area except one. They were truly in love, and surely love conquers all; didn't somebody very wise say that?

Where would they live? When would they go public? So many things to plan. They both agreed that the truth needed to be told to both of their respective partners as soon as they returned home, before any newspapers got wind of it. Both Harry and Malinda deserved at least that much.

Alison and Leo were determined to make the very most of their week together, loving, laughing, enjoying, and growing closer with every passing hour. "Where have you been all my life Alison?" "I was right here Leo, waiting for you to rescue me." Neither of them had ever been happier. Alison thought to herself, well Mom, you will get your grandchild after all, just from a different source. Leo thought to himself, my God, another child at my age, am I being a fool? To hell with it. These are the cards I have been dealt, and I will play this hand to the end, I love this woman. Poor Malinda. It was not going to be plain sailing for either of them. And although neither of them were 'in love' with their partners anymore, they did indeed love and respect them; too many years had passed for them to feel any differently. It was never easy to hurt someone you cared about. But there was no choice.

There were three more days together to go, when the bad weather began. It was all over the news, every hour, updating the coming of Hurricane Cora. It was due to hit in two days. All flights out of Miami were cancelled until further notice as the winds were high and dangerous. Both Leo and Alison called home and filled their respective partners in on the latest development. The storm had bought them a few extra days together. Alison made a booking for a flight home on Aug 4th and Leo arranged his private jet for Aug 5th, back to New York. Both were dreading going home and facing the music, but it had to be done, and now.

Next morning, Leo again had some business to attend to and left Alison happily ensconced in the spare room, composing songs on the piano. She didn't even notice he had gone out.

"Boy oh boy, if I was inspired before," she said out loud, "I am even more inspired now. What great songs this will make. The heartache of separation, the beginning of love, the ending of love... the coming of a baby. Wow... The Heart of Alison. You got that right Oliver, what an album this is going to make. It's all happening. I am in song-writing heaven." As the words and melody began to filter through, she tuned in and began to write:

> 'You've invaded my life, captured my soul
> I'm hooked on your heart, I can't let you go
> You are under my skin, love burns hot, within,
> You've invaded my life, and I can't let you go.
> I'm out of control, so out of control,
> You're are all that I want, and I won't let you go
> No, I can't let you go.
> God I love being,
> Out of control'

Great, she thought, now all I need is a title and a chorus. I quite like 'Out Of Control', because that's exactly how I feel, kinda scary but deliciously scary. Alison tinkled on the piano, playing with different chord structures and melody lines, in her own little creative world. Then she noticed it, a swirling sound, whooshing around the apartment, getting louder and louder. Oh my God... the hurricane!

She quickly went to the living room and switched on the television weather channel. Yep, it's here. Where is Leo? God... I am scared.

Alison sat glued to the set, which was like watching a disaster movie: Cora was being filmed hurtling down the street, bits of trees flying through the air, cars being swept down the road, complete chaos. The weather reporter said, "The worst is just hitting downtown Miami, people have been evacuated from office buildings into the basements, it's now about to hit Fisher Island." Oh my God, thought Alison, Fisher Island, holy shit. And with that there was a crash, and the lights went out.

Leo was at the offices of NBC, talking to the head honcho about next year's schedule for his highly successful talk show 'The King's Court', when the hurricane hit. Alarms went off: evacuate, use the stairs, quickly and quietly came the announcement, and all the employees were led downstairs into the bowels of the high rise building. They could hear the wind roaring on the way down. It was safe down there. All Leo could do was wait with everyone else for the all clear, and get quickly back to Alison. She must be petrified on her own out there, he thought. He didn't realise Cora was about to hit Fisher Island directly, or he would have been petrified himself. He sat on the floor with everyone, determined to calmly wait it out.

Fisher Island had been hit hard. The entire area was in total blackness and the wind was ridiculously strong, uprooting palm trees and smashing windows in shops and houses. Tree branches and small trees were landing on roofs of cars destroying them, rain was pelting down, flooding the streets; Cora had no qualms about attacking the rich in their homes. She would blow and blow until she was finished.

The Hurricane

Alison sat very still on the couch, afraid to move in the darkness. It seemed like she had been there for hours, when in reality it had only been fifteen minutes since the lights went out. I hope Leo is safe wherever he is, she thought. The noise outside was deafening. Suddenly, there was a loud crash as the front door of her apartment was blown off its hinges. She could hear the glass tinkling through the room, and covered her face just in case, and then the door edge hit her. She was knocked to the floor and landed very hard, on her stomach. Then the pain came.. Oh my God, she thought, what's happened? Alison clutched her tummy and rolled into a foetal position. God that hurts, what the hell is happening... she rocked back forth, as each wave of pain came over her, then finally, after about half an hour, there was one big unbearable kick in the guts, then Alison passed out, and the pain subsided.

Just as Alison was coming to, she had some kind of mental flashback. Her mind was in freefall, and all of a sudden she saw her mother - she knew it was her mother - clear as day, she remembered her beautiful mother. They were in a park, and she was pushing her up into the air on a swing, laughing and smiling. Oh my God, the feeling in her heart, she nearly exploded, she could feel her touch, smell her perfume... and then another vision of being thrown up and down and being caught by a strong set of arms, so strong, by a very sweet, good looking young man, her dad. Oh my God Dad, there you are, there we are I remember I remember I remember, then... flying through the air, she remembered this horrible feeling, no control, flung hard and fast... actually flying and landing on the soft ground, then darkness. The accident... finally she could remember, but it was all too much, and she passed out again.

Finally, slowly coming to after about twenty minutes, dazed, she tried to get her bearings, assessing her situation, thankful that at least the pain was gone. What the hell happened? I guess I must be okay, and my God, my memory has returned. Whatever hit me must have jarred something loose. It was only then that she noticed there was something sticky on the floor. The texture and the smell could be nothing else... it was blood, her blood, all over the floor. She felt with her hands around the area and came upon a lump, tiny, but definitely a lump. Oh Jesus Christ, she thought, that's our baby. Gone before it began. She knew it to be true instinctively. Alison stayed where she was, stunned, scared, in pain, sad, and overwhelmed, silent tears rolling down her cheeks. One hour later the lights came back on. Alison was still sitting there, all alone, in the middle of her blood with the tiny lump that had been a human being one hour ago. She couldn't move. She couldn't think. She couldn't do anything but just sit there.

Leo drove back in his limo as soon as they were all released from the basement of the office block. He was nervous as hell seeing the devastation on the streets leading to the apartment; the radio had said Fisher Island took a direct hit. Hurry hurry driver, he thought, hurry... Finally he arrived, and seeing that the front door was ripped off its hinges, he rushed inside not knowing what he would find.

"Oh my God, let her be okay please, please." Glass crunched beneath his shoes, then he spotted her sitting on the floor. Quickly seeing that she was not hurt he said "My sweetness, are you okay, what happened? I got here as soon as I could... are you okay? Speak to me."

Alison stared at him with a vacant look in her eyes. Then slowly she looked down on the ground, her eyes sweeping the bloodied area, and said, "Leo, I have miscarried. Our baby is no more." Only then did she begin to cry, big wrenching sobs for their loss. Leo held her until she stopped. Then he tried the phone, hoping it would work. It did, and he asked maintenance to come and fix the door immediately. He then called a doctor friend in Miami who he trusted and asked him to come over and attend to Alison. Going to a hospital was not an option.

Two hours later, a temporary repair done on the door, and a clean-up in the living room, the doctor arrived with his kit. He took Alison into the bedroom and assessed the situation, examining her for cuts, bruises, and any internal bleeding.

"Miss Heart, I can confirm you have lost your baby. It looks like it was a clean miscarriage obviously caused by you being hit and falling over. I don't think you need to go to the hospital. There is only a small bruise on your hip where the door frame hit you, luckily no glass got into your face. You will probably feel some mood changes in the next few weeks, while your pregnancy hormones leave your body. No harm done. You will be fine."

Fine, thought Alison, you have no idea doctor. She came from the 'everything happens for a reason' school of life, and now everything had changed. She lay there, quietly, teary eyed for her loss, for their loss, teary eyed over the memory of her parents, how wonderful that was... she had been waiting for that memory since she went home and discovered the truth of her birth and young life... teary eyed because it felt like the entire love affair had been through the storm, and maybe it had. This must be some kind of sign, and not a good one.

The doctor cleaned up, said goodbye to Leo, told Alison to take it easy for a couple of days, then left the couple alone.

Without a word, Leo tucked Alison under the covers, got undressed, turned off the light and held her until her sobbing and shaking subsided. Tomorrow... tomorrow they could discuss things; nothing more tonight. Would their love survive this night? The answer was 'blowing in the wind'.

They both awoke around noon. The sun was shining; peaceful, beautiful. Hurricane Cora had done its damage and had moved on.

"I'll get us some coffee my sweetness, you stay put. The doctor says you must rest all day. Then, I suggest we both call our respective partners to put them at their ease and then we must talk about our future."

"Okay Leo, I will call Harry now while you're making the coffee. Why don't you call your wife from the other room? Then we both have some privacy."

Alison dialled the long distance number and heard the ring, strangely unfamiliar all of a sudden.

"Hello? Alison, is that you? I have been watching the news all night long, are you okay? Isn't Fisher Island where you are staying? Hello? Hello... speak to me... I have been so worried."

"Yes Harry, I am fine. All the lines were out last night or I would have phoned you." (That was a little white lie that did no-one any harm.) "Miami airport will be open again the day after tomorrow so I will book on the first flight out and let you know the details. You don't have to come to the airport, just send a limo. It was so scary, never been in a hurricane before and don't wish to be in one again." (My life is now one big hurricane, she thought, it's a storm waiting to happen.) "I'll call now and get back to you with the details. Love you. Bye."

And in the other room Leo was talking.

"Hello darling. Yes, yes, I am fine. Horrible... yep... debris everywhere. I was stuck downtown in the office when it hit. Yes, yes, don't worry, I am fine, absolutely fine." (I am anything but fine, he thought.) "I will call Tony, he will know when the airport will be open again. Probably in a day or so. See you soon. I'll let you know as soon as I know. Bye for now."

They met in the living room, and sat on the couch, at opposite ends. Alison looked long and hard at Leo. No-one spoke for about ten minutes. Finally she broke the silence.

"So, the unexpected situation that dictated that we must be together is now no more. We are under no obligation to commit to this relationship for the sake of a baby. In one way, I am devastated to have lost our child, but in another, relieved that we now appear to have a choice. Do we ruin lives, do we take a chance, should we take a chance, is our love strong enough to stand all the hurt and guilt that will come our way when we divorce? I don't know any more. I just don't know. Maybe it's just my

185

hormones speaking, maybe it's the shock, who knows... and of course you must be aware that the media will have a feeding frenzy once our relationship gets out. I am definitely reconsidering my position." For a woman Alison was being extremely logical, but that was always one of her strengths. She thought like a man, with the emotions of a woman: a deadly combination.

There was a pause.

"How do you feel Leo?"

Leo took his moment, lit a rare cigarette and started to pace around the living room. "My sweetness," he finally began, "I have been around the block and back again, I have done the marriage, the family, the grandkids, the whole shebang. Yes, last night has given me cause to reconsider our predicament. There is only one thing I am sure of, and that is that I love you, and in fact am in love for the first time in my entire life and I do not want to let that go. I am willing to take this chance... I am willing to marry you."

"What?" Alison's mouth dropped open. "Are you really asking me to marry you? I'm not even divorced yet. My God Leo... are you sure?"

"Yes, I am." Leo dropped to one knee, took Alison's hand and repeated, directly into her eyes: "Will you marry me and make me the happiest man on earth?"

All logic went out the window. "Yes yes yes yes yes," she said, and they sealed their commitment in a hour of tender lovemaking. Oh my God, thought Alison, if this is heaven, open the gate, I'm coming in. Oh my God, thought Leo, I was starving and I didn't even know it. Happy? You bet.

It was finally time for them both to go home and face the music. Alison's flight was in the evening and Leo's was first thing in the morning the next day, his being a private jet with Tony in the pilot's seat. They said their goodbyes. Alison rolled her bag out, got in the limo and drove to the airport, deep in thought.

How am I am going to approach this? I don't know where to begin. I guess, in all fairness, I will have to tell Harry everything. I am dreading it. He will be destroyed. But truth is the only way forward. And I've only got about ten hours to get it all together. Shit.

With these thoughts, Alison boarded the flight home. Sleep did not come.

Harry did book a limo, but decided to travel to the airport with the car. He did not want to wait. He wanted to greet his beautiful wife as soon as she came through customs. God, he had missed her. She still had that effect on him. She was the love of his life and that would never change. He showered, washed his hair, brushed his teeth, poured on some cologne, put on his tightest blue-jeans with black

Cuban heeled leather boots, a clean white t-shirt, and his Levi jacket. Harry's fashion sense had never changed: he liked what he liked and he looked good in it. And Alison never complained.

They arrived at the terminal. He instructed the driver to wait, went inside the arrival hall, checked the electronic list on the wall, saw that the plane had landed five minutes ago, went to the end of where the passengers would come out, and waited for his beloved. Ten, fifteen, twenty minutes dragged by, and then he saw her, being led by an airport official, looking beautiful as always, rolling her little case behind her.

My darling, there she is. Harry ran to her and enveloped her in a big bear hug, squeezing the life out of her. "God I missed you darlin', so much." He felt her stiffen slightly, and wondered briefly what was wrong, but quickly pushed any questions out of his mind, putting it down to jet lag. "Hello Harry, I missed you too," Alison replied automatically. Hand in hand they walked to the limo.

"I am absolutely shattered darling, I didn't sleep a wink on the flight back. It was too bumpy." Putting on her sleeping mask, she was out like a light until they hit Essex. There was no conversation on the way home, or that whole day, which Alison spent unpacking and lazing around in her jet lag, trying hard not to think of anything. Tomorrow, tomorrow, she thought, I'll do it tomorrow.

The Hurricane

Falling asleep early, she awoke around 3am, with a snoring Harry beside her. Not wanting to disturb him, she went downstairs for a glass of wine, and distractedly switched on the television. She began to channel surf.

I must tell Harry everything, first thing in the morning, she thought. Leo will be home by now. This emotional explosion cannot be delayed any more. Decision made, she faced the inevitable in her mind: this marriage was over. Slowly she sipped her wine, going over how she would begin, what she would say, how she would react once Harry started to cry, or even worse, once he stared to beg. Oh God, she thought, how can I be so cruel? Damn it Leo, you changed the game. I wasn't looking for you. I was happy or anyway, I thought I was happy... damn.

Just then the word 'Newsflash' flicked across the screen, interrupting the program. Alison turned the volume up.

"TV talk show host Leo King has died in a plane crash shortly after leaving Miami airport. He was travelling in a private Lear jet. There was no Mayday reported and investigators are trying to discover the cause of the accident. The pilot and Mr King died instantly when the plane plunged to the ground about ten minutes after take-off. Mr King leaves his wife, four children and six grandchildren. His wife and family are unavailable for comment.

Stay tuned for the latest update on this tragic accident. Tributes have been pouring in from all over the world from stars who have been interviewed by him through the years. He was respected and loved by one and all and will be sadly missed in the industry."

A picture of the burning wreckage filled the screen. Alison was speechless, absolutely speechless. Oh my dear God, she mouthed silently, as a stream of tears ran down her face. Thank God Harry was asleep; she could never talk her way out of this.

She sat on the couch for the rest of the night. It was a long, long night. She was in a daze, trying to take it all in, and finally, as the sun rose over the Essex countryside, she had made her decision. She would not react with histrionics; she would let no-one know anything at all, not about Leo, not about the miscarriage, not even about her discovery of her true beginnings. These would be her secrets to bear, her secrets to take to her grave. Harry had been given a reprieve and would never know it. 'Everything happens for a reason' was Alison's mantra, and it had never been more true than at this very moment in her life. She would shelve everything way back in the corner of her heart. Life did go on and would go on.

For the next four months Alison wrote and wrote and wrote. She had almost too much inspiration. The heartache was flowing out with every word she wrote, the pain with every note she sang, the loss with every chord she struck. She was like a woman possessed, working all day in her music room, only coming out for a meal, then working again until bedtime. When Harry questioned her, she simply said, "Leave me be honey, I just need to get this done, and it's flowing good. We are in the studio soon. Be patient." What he didn't know wouldn't hurt him.

Every now and again they had one sided sex, which was the best Alison could do. Harry, if he noticed, wisely said nothing. She was hoping against hope that she would eventually be able to fall back in love, but the reality was that that train had gone. For the moment, she would just write, write and write, which enabled her to focus on something... but Leo, Leo, Leo, forever in her thoughts, and now forever gone. How cruel to fall in love that deeply then have it snatched away. Maybe it would have been better to never have met, she mused, but then immediately replaced that thought with, No... at least I had that once in my life, and I will take the love we shared to my grave. I love you Leo, wherever you are. Then she went back to the piano, a sheet of paper, a pencil and her heartache.

Chapter Twenty-Two

The Heart of Alison

It was finally time to begin recording her new album. She went into the studio armed with the very best original songs of her entire career, and she had written a few gems in her time at the top. She had used the entire last year and a half, with all its tragedies, as a prelude to creation. She was turning this around into something positive, honouring her real mother and father, her unborn child and the love of her life, Leo King. Honouring her secrets. She always had artistic licence to fall back on. The list of song titles said it all.

No Choice
Out Of Control
The Roar Of The Jungle
Who Am I?
Home Is A Four Letter Word

Love Lives, Love Dies (her favourite, because
nobody would get it but her)
Where Are You, Baby?
Forgive Me
True To You
Keep On Walking
Don't Look Back

Harry had approached the song subject a few
times with questions like, "Where did this lyric
come from?" and "Who is this about?" and "What
the hell is going on? Boy you are on a roll" and "This
is deep good stuff darling but it's certainly not your
normal" and "Are you sure the fans are going to
accept this kind of music from you?" The sixty four
thousand dollar question was "What happened to the
Alison Heart that I fell in love with?" but he kept
that question to himself. He was going along for the
ride, trying to be helpful, trying to be her partner,
but aware, someplace deep inside, that he would
never be her 'partner' again. If Harry suspected there
had been or was somebody else, he kept these
thoughts suppressed, where they could not surface.
In reality he did not want to know the answer. He
was the proverbial ostrich, head in the sand. All that
matters, he thought, is my wife is by my side.

Oliver, who absolutely loved Alison's new
direction, had booked an impressive roster of
musicians, ones who had the chops and could

interpret these hauntingly beautiful songs. They had a four week open ended booking at Abbey Road, the best of the best. She had, for the first time, written them all on piano, and not on guitar. "It is not mine to question," Oliver said to Alison, sitting in his office, discussing the album, "But I tell you my little rock star, this is award winning stuff. Whatever happened, I don't want to know either, but it has really tuned you on to the creativity inside. In fact, it has awakened the 'female' in you, and it's delicious. I knew you were talented, I never knew you were this talented. Let's go make a hit album, shall we?" And they did.

In 1980, 'The Heart Of Alison' was finally released and rocketed up to the top position on the album charts in several countries; the critics raved, the fans rejoiced, everyone was happy, and nobody seemed to mind her change of direction, in fact just the opposite. "Alison grows up"..."Rock chick bears all"... "Dive into this diva folks, she is the real deal"... That was how the critics were writing about this new offering. If possible, she was even bigger than before. A tour was planned, a tour with a difference, lots of stuff done just on piano with backing vocals, and then growing into full orchestra ending with the rock band sound she was famous for. It would be the tour of her life, literally. Alison was in artistic heaven - God, how she loved creation.

Although it made the pain a little easier to bear, she still thought about him every single day.

Alison spent her days planning the set list, planning her outfits, choosing her musicians, and getting fit. This was essential: jogging, gym, yoga, nonstop. She was a busy, busy girl with no time to dwell on anything unpleasant, which suited her right down to the ground. She and Harry were rocking and rolling along as they settled into a kind of routine that didn't require any deep conversation about anything. It was a day to day existence, neither here nor there. She wasn't unhappy with him, just not happy: it was love limbo. Hey, she thought, that's another good title, maybe for the next album. Life went on.

Early one morning, around 8:30, the phone rang in Mr and Mrs Pullman aka Mr and Mrs Heart's house. Alison answered immediately; she wasn't sleeping too well lately and was always up with the birds. "Hello?"

It was Oliver. "Hello my little rock star. I have some news for you. Do you remember that talk show you did in New York when 'Ballbust Her' came out with Leo King, God rest his soul?"

"Yes, God rest his soul," Alison retorted before she could stop herself.

"Well, they have revamped it, with a new compere, made it more 'entertainment' friendly, not just interviews. The new host's name is J J Coleman, known as JJ." Oh my God, Alison thought, I can guess what's coming. "Anyway, they have requested your presence next week to do a song live..." Yep, she thought, I knew it. Can I go back there, to the same studio, the same show, albeit a different host, can I?

"They want 'Love Lives Love Dies', and an interview. I can book you you on a flight immediately, let's say two days before the show, then stay on a couple more, Warwick hotel, usual suite?"

Damn it, she thought, yes I can. I have to face my demons sooner or later, and maybe doing this song, which is one million percent our song, will help me come to terms with everything, truly come to terms. Alison's thought processes were moving at lightning speed. Oliver continued, not aware of anything amiss, "You'll go alone. I need Harry here next week. Listen to me. At the moment, the new album is sitting at number 10 in Billboard, Cashbox and Record World. This could push it all the way home, and we could get a Grammy nomination if we make the top spot. This album deserves it. We need this show. What do you say... green light?"

Alison paused briefly, clearing her throat. "Yep, you're on Oliver. I could do with a quick fix of New York City."

Chapter Twenty-Three

Malinda King

In New York, Malinda King was preparing herself for another meaningless day. She had begun to drink more and more after Leo had died. Not her kids, nor her grandchildren, could lift her up. Not even the alcohol helped any more, but at least it numbed her a little bit. It had been over a year and a half now but the pain was still as fresh as the day it happened. Time Heals she thought, what crap! She lay in bed for a while, thinking about how everything had changed so drastically. Will I ever be happy again?

She rose slowly, dressed herself, put on some makeup - Malinda was always immaculate in her appearance - went to the kitchen, poured some coffee, sat at the table, lit a cigarette, and wondered how in hell she would get through another day. But she did, somehow.

She cut a sad lonely figure sitting in her beautiful kitchen with the sunlight streaming through the window, sunlight that could not reach her dark broken heart. She had loved Leo very much, that was a fact. She had no desire for anyone else, and sometimes, when she remembered their happier times together, she went into such a blue funk that she actually considered doing a quick exit from this world that had no meaning anymore. Oh yes, she was depressed, with a capital D. Poor Malinda, could nothing ease her plight? It seemed not.

Later that evening, after a day of mindless shopping and buying of goods she didn't need, Malinda poured herself the first glass of vintage Krug, her favourite. She would finish the bottle. Lazing around on their sumptuous couch - at least he had left her well provided for - she was watching television without really watching, robotically switching from channel to channel trying to find something, anything, to catch her interest, when her prayers were answered.

"Ladies and Gentleman, welcome to..." (music fanfare) "...the all new 'The Happening', the best entertainment show on t.v... starring J J Coleman... and here he is...."

Oh my God, thought Malinda. This is the show that took over from Leo's. Well, I may as well watch. There was huge applause as a man, around fiftyish but looking good on it, blonde, tall and slim, took the stage, running through his opening one liners. The studio audience clapped, jeered and laughed just like a studio audience always did, predictable but necessary for the ratings. Gags over, JJ, as he was known, sat down behind his desk and began the introduction for who was on the show that evening.

"Tonight we have upcoming comic, Dan Diamond, Oscar winning actress, Kate Hughes, author, Dan Fields, but first - Gosh, I am so so excited to have her on my show - Please welcome, the delectable, the gorgeous, the talented, the wonderful... Miss Alison Heart, doing a song from her new album, 'The Heart Of Alison' - the album and the single both destined for the top of the charts - here she is with 'Love Lives Love Dies.'"

Malinda watched Alison, sitting at the piano, gently but emotionally singing the song. Slowly she was drawn into the lyrics, and it all came flooding back: Leo's talk show, 1978, their interview, together, her real worry that this girl was a threat to her marriage. Then, before she could even explore this fear, fate had stepped in and Leo was gone. Funny, she had never thought about Alison or her fears since then. It seemed so unimportant after the plane crash, which took precedence over everything, until tonight, seeing Alison Heart doing her new song on television. Something was niggling her, and she couldn't quite put her finger on it. She sat there glued to the set until the interview ended.

The Hurricane

JJ began: "So Miss Heart, thank you for joining us tonight. What a great song, what a great album. I hear a rumour that you're are going to be nominated for a Grammy... and you heard it first here folks..."

Alison took her applause graciously, smiling in return. "Thank you JJ, I am glad to be here." There was the normal blah blah blah back and forth, and Malinda nearly switched off; then JJ asked, "The question I'm sure all your fans are asking, and I know I would like to know the answer too Alison, if I may call you that, is, where the hell did the inspiration for these songs come from? They are not anything like your normal material. What did you do, have an illicit affair or something?" JJ splurted out, laughing out loud, thinking he was being very funny and daring at the same time.

The silence was deafening. Alison actually blushed deep red, and the camera panned in. Damn, she was thinking, I have never been a good liar... Boy oh boy, that caught me off guard, get your shit together girl. And she did, gathering her wits about her and finally answering in her best rock chick 'attitude' voice: "Oh come on JJ, I am a happily married woman, have been for many years. I have simply grown up a bit and taken my writing to the next natural level. But if I do want an affair, believe me... you'd be the last one I would contact." She played to the cameras with a twinkle in her eye. Now it was JJ's turn to blush.

The Hurricane

The very next day, Malinda went out and bought the album.

Alone in the Kings' movie/stereo room, with all the best equipment and most comfortable seats - they enjoyed so many wonderful evenings here - Malinda put the album on the turntable. She sat on the couch, glass of Krug ready and waiting, opened up the sleeve so she could follow the lyrics as she listened, and began the journey. The opening track was the single 'Love Lives Love Dies', and the words seemed to reach out and grab her right by the heart.

> I wasn't looking for anyone
> When you invaded my life
> Just a couple of star crossed lovers
> I had a husband, you had a wife
> We took a trip towards ecstasy
> Destination still unknown
> But fate would have its say oh yes,
> And I would end up all alone.
>
> Love lives love dies
> You're in my heart and in my soul
> Love lives love dies
> I will never let you go
> You are forever alive
> In my heart and in my soul
> Love lives love dies

No, I will never ever let you go.

Each song told its own story, and every song, without fail, was about uncontrollable love, and loss. It was a marvellous work of music, very intelligent, very sensitive, beautifully played, and it really tugged at your heart strings. Then, all of a sudden, the light went on.

"Oh my God," Malinda said out loud. "Oh my God, now it makes sense." Leo had been so distant after that interview with Alison Heart; she remembered watching them straining towards each other, thinking how intimate it all looked even in the harsh lights of a television studio. Even when I attacked him sexually in the shower, thought Malinda, the memory bringing a brief smile to her face, it was only half hearted, in fact half hard would be more appropriate. I knew then, I just ignored it, damn: they had an affair. I am absolutely sure of it. It's all there in the songs, and it all makes sense. That trip to Miami, damn, that trip to Miami, I just knew something wasn't kosher with it. I begged him to let me go... and those ridiculous excuses he came up with, and that phone call telling me the airport was closed, sounding like my husband, yet not. I knew something was up. Something serious. I felt then like I had lost him, but couldn't figure out why I thought that. Now I know, or at least I think I know. I could be wrong... but no, I don't think I am. She must have been there with him, must have been. This album confirms it. God, this will drive me crazy unless I can piece together what happened. Then maybe I can grieve properly and finally bury him.

After sitting there a little while longer, her mind was finally made up. I will get in touch with Miss Alison Heart, she decided. I will meet her. I will find the truth. I need to know if they had an affair, I need to know if they loved each other, I need to know if he was going to divorce me, I need to know. Only then will I find my peace.

Malinda still had all her contacts at NBC, so the next morning she made a few phone calls, found out where Ms Heart was staying, and dialled the number.

"Hello, I'd like to speak to Ms Alison Heart. I believe she is in the Cary Grant suite."

"Yes, and who shall I say is phoning?" said the twangy voiced operator.

"Miss Malinda King."

Alison answered the phone, heard who was on the other end of the line, and made a snap decision. "Fine, put her through please." Well, she thought, this should be interesting.

"Hello Alison, if I may call you that. I feel as if know you already. This is Leo King's widow, Malinda King."

"Yes, please do call me Alison. First can I say how sorry I am about your husband's death, it was a shock to the world. He was very well loved." Especially by me, she thought. "What can I do for you?"

"Well, I would very much like to meet up for lunch. Leo always spoke very highly of you and it would be nice to actually say hello, especially now that my husband is no longer with us." She was keeping her true agenda to herself.

Alison was thinking quickly - yes or no, yes or no - and then:

"Of course Malinda. It would be a pleasure. How about meeting me in the Italian restaurant which is right next door to the reception at the Warwick? Is 1pm convenient tomorrow? I leave for London the next day."

The deal was done. What tomorrow's lunch would bring, neither of them knew, but both were curious.

Alison awoke the next morning feeling refreshed yet apprehensive. Maybe I should have refused, she thought to herself, but why? My God, the poor woman. She was his wife after all. Alison washed her hair, and while it was drying naturally ordered apple juice and strong black coffee, snuggled up nicely in the thick white terry cloth robe the suite provided. She pottered around, packing a few bits and pieces for tomorrow's flight, until it was 12:15. Then she started to get ready.

A little mascara, a little lightener under the eyes, a little green eye shadow to bring her eyes out, just a little blush, and a natural looking lipstick. Her long hair hung loose and free down her back. "Now, what to wear... do I go as a rock chick or do I dress a little more demure?" Rock chick won out. Alison Heart needs to be in charge of this lunch, she thought, and Alison Heart had better not give anything away. Ready. Here we go.

Alison got there five minutes early, as it should be, so that Mrs. King would not have to sit alone. She knew it was her as soon as she appeared in the doorway, dressed in a light blue Chanel fitted skirt and jacket, white silk blouse, white expensive pearls, diamond ring and bracelet, Cartier watch, beige nylons and blue heels, with perfectly coiffed hair; confident and in charge was how she walked in to the restaurant. We're like chalk and cheese, Alison mused as she rose to greet her.

There was an awkward moment as they eyed each other up, both thinking their own thoughts, both guarded, both curious, then they gently shook hands and sat down. The lunch had begun.

"So, Alison, may I call you that?"

"No problem, and may I call you Malinda?"

"You must be wondering why I wanted to meet you; after all, there really is no reason. After all, you only met my husband that one time on his television show, so what could we possibly have to talk about, right?" Malinda looked directly in her eyes, and saw the truth.

She knows, thought Alison.

I'm right, thought Malinda.

Just then the waiter appeared to take their drinks order, thank goodness, giving them both time to collect themselves. "Would you like some champagne Malinda? I believe you like Krug don't you?" Whoops, thought Alison, how would I know that?

Malinda let that one pass by, and said, "Yes, I do, and that's fine."

Neither said a word until the champagne was brought to the table in an ice bucket, opened and poured. They clinked glasses and the afternoon began.

The lunch lasted over three hours. Malinda asked the right questions and Alison found herself warming to her. She was a very nice woman, refined and a little boring, but nice. They talked about everything under the sun. Alison told her about her life at the top of the music business, how she had survived it, about Harry, how they met, about Oliver and how they met, about Cleveland, in fact, all about her life, stopping short at her being adopted, but only just. She felt the need to bear her soul to this woman for some crazy reason. Maybe it was the Leo connection.

Malinda was very attentive and interested. Then it was her turn: she filled Alison in on how she and Leo met, their children, their grandchildren, the deep love they had for each other, and how she was coping now that he was gone. The champagne and the conversation flowed easily, both of them finding their tongues were getting very loose indeed and not a little slurred around the edges, and, it must be said, Alison was a little more tipsy than Malinda; after all Malinda had a lot more practice at this champagne lark.

Finally, Malinda asked the questions she had been trying to ask all afternoon, shot straight out with no warning, like bullets.

"Alison, did you have an affair with my husband?"

"Yes, I did."

"Did you go to Miami with him on that fatal trip?"

"Yes I did."

"Did you love him?"

"Yes I did."

"Did he love you?"

"Yes he did."

"Were you planning on marrying?"

"Yes we were."

Quietly, and in a respectful voice, Alison continued.

"And, Malinda, since I am telling you the truth, straight up, one more thing you should know, I was pregnant. I miscarried during the hurricane. We were both going to tell our partners when we returned home that we wanted a divorce. Of course that never happened with Leo, and it never happened with me. I decided after hearing the news of the crash on television that nobody need know anything.

"This will be our secret. We will always share the love we both had for your husband. What the future may have held, who knows?"

They looked at each other a long time... and then at the same time, smiled, real smiles from the heart. "Cheers to Leo," said Malinda. "Yes, cheers to Leo," said Alison, and they clinked glasses and the bond between them was sealed. They would be friends, good friends from that moment on. Funny how life turns out, isn't it?

They exchanged phone numbers and promised to keep in touch. In fact, they both needed each other to keep Leo's memory alive. Alison caught her flight out the next morning, deep in thought all the way back to England. Talking with Malinda had brought Leo right back to the front of her mind, and heart. I hope I can keep up the facade, she thought. I mean, I know I am not in love with Harry anymore, but hell, what is the alternative? It's called Alone, because after Leo, well, there is no after Leo... what a man he was. So, let's just go home and keep the charade going. I'll know when it's time to move on, and it's not yet. And time went on.

Chapter Twenty-Four

1981

Alison, after fleeing her life with Harry, had been ensconced in the Warwick Hotel for over five days now, doing nothing but remembering, crying, thinking, trying to decide what she wanted to do with the rest of her life. She knew, without a shadow of a doubt, that she had to leave Harry, and that she had to come clean with him. Morality demanded it. And maybe the truth would toughen him up enough to be able to deal with the divorce. She made the call.

Luckily the machine answered.

"Hello Harry, it's me. I am ready to come back now, so please have Oliver book me on Concorde, leaving tomorrow. We can talk when I get home. Bye."

Chapter Twenty-Five

Back Home

Back in Bocking, Essex, that first night home, Alison was able to feign tiredness, promising that the next day they would sit and discuss their future. And then it was the next day. No more delays, she thought, the truth, and nothing but the truth, so help me God... here we go.

They sat in their classically decorated front room, in front of the beautiful original stone fireplace, on opposite couches, facing each other, with a roaring fire going, and a nice old Margaux, one of her favourite wines.

"Harry, do me a favour, say nothing. I need to get this all out in one go. Please. Okay, first of all:

I had an affair with Leo King.

I fell in love with Leo King.

I was pregnant by Leo King.

I didn't know this when I went to Miami, not until I got there and worked out the dates. During

211

the hurricane I got hit by a door frame, and lost the baby. We were planning on getting married. I was planning on telling you as soon as I got back. Then, of course, the plane crash. I decided to keep my secret to myself. There was no point in ruining your life, when the life I was planning was not even possible anymore.

Also..." She was rushing ahead with her words...

"When I went back to Cleveland to see my folks, I found out..." She was gulping and choking up. "I ffffound out... shit this is hard...

I found out that my real mother and father were killed in a car crash.

I was thrown out of the car, and suffered memory loss, and was unconscious for about a week. I was just over four years old.

They put me in a foster home as there were no known living relatives.

I was finally adopted by Mom and Dad Heart.

My real name is Alison Cunningham not Alison Heart.

My adoptive parents planned on telling me one day.

That day never came.

Then I went back to Cleveland, after my first time with Leo, and it was at this point I discovered by accident my true beginnings. I now know everything about who I am. I even had a real memory of my parents, when I got hit by that door in Florida during Hurricane Cora. I finally know who I am Harry... after all these years, I finally know who I am. Alison Meredith Heart, the girl, the rock star, the person you fell in love with, is not who I am. I am little Alison Cunningham, and I have been searching for me for my entire life. Phew, okay... that's everything."

Alison paused and had a sip of her wine, gathering her courage around her. The fire crackled in the background, the flames lighting up Harry's inscrutable face. He was in shock, and just sat there still and in complete silence. She continued:

"I have tried to put everything behind me. I wanted to carry on with you, I did carry on with you, for the last three years, because we are good together, we are friends, we are close, and I do love you... but after Leo, shit I am so sorry Harry, after Leo, there could be no going back. What I felt for him... my true love, my true soulmate, well, it changed everything. The reason I escaped to New York was that I finally reached the end of this pretence. I can't do it anymore, I just can't. I am telling you now, without question..." She said the next four words quietly, but with strength. "I want a divorce. I am so sorry." She didn't cry.

There was no pleading, there was no recrimination, there was nothing. Harry just stared at Alison with a dead look in his eyes, as one lone tear rolled down his whiskered lined face. Eventually he got up, took his empty glass of wine to the kitchen, poured himself a large whiskey and took his joint tin upstairs, retiring for the evening, leaving Alison sitting by herself, alone, in front of the fire, alone, alone, alone. I've done it, and the truth has set me free, she thought to herself. Or maybe not.

She didn't know how long she sat there. Eventually dawn started to peek around the edges of the night. The fire had died out - now that's an analogy, she thought - and she rose to go and make herself a cup of coffee.

The shot, when it came, reverberated through the house. Oh my God, no no no no... she ran as quickly as her legs could carry her, taking the stairs two at a time, petrified of what awaited her in their bedroom. She flung open the oak door. He had jammed a rifle under the bedroom chair so it was pointing straight up, attached a string to the trigger, stood over it and... and shot himself. His body was lying on the floor, motionless; what was left of his head was expressionless; Harry was one million percent dead. He would feel no more pain.

Alison buried her husband in the cemetery specified in his Will. It was an unusually sunny day for England. The birds were singing, the flowers were blooming, and everything looked beautiful as they lowered his casket into the ground. She had put in the coffin a bottle of his favourite whiskey, his favourite gold chain that she had bought for him, a picture of them together in The Rough Edges, and the guitar clock her mother had given her all those years ago. "Your time has run out my love." It was a very small funeral: Oliver was there, a couple of distant relatives were there, two or three friends, and Bo Bo from the old band had flown over; and Daniella O'Donnel, her real mom's best friend, had somehow scraped enough money to fly over. Alison's mom and dad had come as well. But the big surprise was Malinda King. They had kept in contact since that lunch, and Alison was so touched that she had made the effort. She was a true friend. Once the final blessings had been made, everyone began to go back up the hill to the local pub where the wake would take place. Alison lagged behind wanting a few quiet private moments with her thoughts. Everyone respected that and walked ahead.

Standing over the fresh earth that had been piled upon the coffin, she let her emotions flow, and the words came easily; she said them out loud, knowing Harry could hear her, without a shadow of a doubt.

"Goodbye my Harry, goodbye to you my best friend. You will always be my Harry. My God, we had quite a life together didn't we? You were a good man, one of the best, and I did love you very very much. Never doubt that. I am so sorry for the heartache of the last few years, it was beyond my control. You are at peace now. Rest easy, my sweet sweet man. I will always keep you in my heart. I love you." And then she sobbed like a baby. When she was done, she trudged up the hill to join everyone else. Another chapter closed.

Chapter Twenty-Six

1982

A year had gone by since Alison had buried her husband, and four years had gone by since Leo King had been killed in that plane crash. Alison had stopped touring, stopped writing, stopped doing everything. She became a recluse in her manor house in the Essex countryside. She needed some time out to address the tragic twists and turns her life had taken. Being a rock star didn't seem so important anymore.

What she now needed to do was take stock of her real life without the trappings of success. She floundered for quite a few months, not knowing who she was, where she was going, or what she wanted. Emotionally she was as naked as the day she was born. A lot of time was spent going through old photos, watching videos, leafing through the scrapbook Mom and Dad Heart had given her at the funeral, listening to early recordings of The Rough

Edges, watching that interview with Leo King, over and over again, and making a few calls to Malinda, who was always helpful and supportive. But in the end, she only had herself. I have to pull myself together, she thought. Life goes on... life must go on... life will go on... and she hummed the song her mother had taught her all those years ago with the hint of a smile playing at the corners of her mouth.

"Que sera sera, whatever will be will be, the future's not ours to see, que sera sera, what will be will be..."

Amen.

Chapter Twenty-Seven

Alison Creates

The Hurricane

Lyric ideas ②
(mid tempo - Key G)
on piano

You've invaded my ~~soul~~ life
Captured my soul
I'm hooked on your heart
) ~~Can't~~ let you go
Won't

You are under my skin
Love burns hot, within
You've invaded my life
Now I can't let you go

I'm out of control
So damn out of control
You're all that I want
& I just won't let you go
No I can't let you go

Fad I love being
Out of control ← title?

feel chorus
maybe use this

220

③ The Roar of the Jungle

(live drum loop — odd jungle noises —
use sparse chording — every 3 bars only
rhythm + lyric must carry song)
more spoken than sung

idea for lyrics:

the roar of the jungle
the devils delight
who knows if my lion
will sleep tonight
the roar of the jungle
is loud + clear
who knows if _my_ lions
intentions are pure

chorus % 4x over drums
    the roar of the jungle

④   Who Am I   Key Am

(notes to self — think Mary & David,
how would they have done it —
lullaby style - picked acoustic
guitar — start with chorus)

Safe in your arms
I'm so warm in your arms
Please hold me forever
in your hearts, in your hearts
Safe in your love
Send me warmth from above
And I'll hold you forever
in my heart, in my heart

_____

verse goes here
↳

The Hurricane

5 Home — A 4 letter word   Key E

(do rough edges style — write on guitar)
(note to self — lots to do on the one!)

Its a place I've never known
Since forever, a gypsy, I ROAM
~~About~~ Damn it to hell!
Theres so much to tell
Where is my home —
where is my home —
+ why must I be — alone!!

(phew — dig deep on this Alison —
    So the distance)
      G

Later — (this is a
      midnight song!)

⑥ <u>LOVE LIVES, LOVE DIES</u>   Key Am

Solo piano + vox + nothing else!
maybe bv's — notes for production

I wasn't looking for anyone
When you invaded my life (no no's)
Just a couple of star crossed lovers
I <u>had</u> a husband, you had a wife

We took a trip to ecstacy
destination.... still unknown (yeah yeah)
But fate would have it say oh yes
& I would end up <u>Alone</u>

        Chorus

love lives, love dies
Your in my ~~heart~~ + in my soul
love live love dies
& I will never let you go
~~You are~~ forever alive
in my heart + in my soul
love lives love dies
<u>no no</u> ~~I~~ will never, never, never
        let you go
*(C maybe okay for Chorus)

The Hurricane

① <u>Where are you baby?</u>
(Light production, too heavy to sound heavy!)

BASIC <u>concept</u>

2 people in love
2 people <u>Both</u> taken
A BABY — then, a baby no more
<u>Smiles + tears</u>
<u>Must decide</u> Song or poem?

Maybe just a poem after all
a line in <u>my life!</u>

(work on this too)

8   FORGIVE ME   (For HARRY, PooR BABY)

Verse
It was my turn to roll the dice
It was my game, guess I didn't think twice
It was your pain — these cards you were dealt
May be my gain, But oh, the guilt I felt

Chorus
Forgive me
I cant need you, anymore
Forgive me
I cant want you, anymore
Forgive me
No one can even this score
Forgive me
We're not lovers anymore

need 1 verse + Bridge
To Chorus + Fade

The Hurricane

⑨ <u>True To You</u>   Key G
      Voice + strings only
                    (try #)

I was true to you
for such a <u>long</u> time

I was through with you
But <u>these</u> thoughts were mine

I tried, ~~I tried~~ how I tried
I cried, God how I cried

I was true to you
But now that love has died

(simple but effective

The Hurricane

(10) Keep on Walking
(Don't Look Back)
(Motown Bassline — Cool Tempo — Rumbling!)

Key A

Chorus

Keep on Walking, don't look Back
Keep on Walking — don't look Back
No more talking, that's enough of that
Keep on walking — don't look Back

Verse (note — start with verse not chorus)

I had a Dream
The other Night
I was alone again
and my world was right
but when I awoke —
You were licing next to me
then I realized —
I had to break free
oh yes I just had to Break free

(chorus break into
Big Chorus)

228

About the Author

Suzi Quatro has been a household name since 1973, when she screamed her way into the public consciousness with her first No. 1 record, Can The Can. Long before The Spice Girls were even a twinkle in their mothers' eyes, Suzi was the original Girl Power icon. She kicked open the door for all the female lead singers of the past four decades. Suzi went on to sell 55 million records, star alongside The Fonz in Happy Days, take the title role in the stage version of Annie Get Your Gun and host her own long-running BBC Radio 2 series.

Today Suzi lives with her husband Rainer near Chelmsford in the UK. Their love-match is celebrated in her book Through My Eyes' final poem: You Are My Dream Come True.

Suzi received an honorary doctorate of music from the Anglia Ruskin University in Cambridge in 2016. Dr Suzi is penning more titles for New Haven and is still constantly on tour and making appearances all over the world.

The Hurricane